Honeymoon for One

CHRIS KENISTON

Indie House Publishing

BOOKS BY CHRIS KENISTON

Hart Land
Heather
Lily
Violet
Iris
Hyacinth
Rose
Calytrix
Zinnia
Poppy

Farraday Country
Adam
Brooks
Connor
Declan
Ethan
Finn
Grace
Hannah
Ian
Jamison
Keeping Eileen
Loving Chloe
Morgan

Aloha Series Heartwarming Edition:
Aloha Texas
Almost Paradise
Mai Tai Marriage
Dive Into You
Look of Love
Love by Design
Love Walks In

Shell Game
Flirting with Paradise

Surf's Up Flirts:
(Aloha Series Companions)
Shall We Dance
Love on Tap
Head Over Heels
Perfect Match
Just One Kiss
It Had to Be You

Honeymoon Series
Honeymoon for One
Honeymoon for Three
Honeymoon for Four

Other Books
By Chris Keniston

Family Secrets Novels:
Champagne Sisterhood
The Homecoming
Hope's Corner

ACKNOWLEDGMENTS

With every story no matter how long or short I have my stable of loyal colleagues and friends who I turn to for support, encouragement, and of course, correction.

My thanks to Linda Steinberg for brainstorming any time of day or night. Adrienne Giordano and her husband for feeding me all the challenges of saving—or killing—a newspaper. Any and all mistakes are mine.

Since nothing could get me to climb a rock wall, my thanks to Sarah Cress for sharing the experience. And a special thank you to Cheryl Lucas for making every vacation a spring board for a new book. Long may we travel!

CHAPTER ONE

Something wasn't right. Michelle Bradford stared at her cell phone. To a stranger, her best friend since kindergarten might sound perfectly normal, but Michelle could hear the slight edge in Beth's voice. The hitch in her breath.

A knot tightened in the pit of Michelle's stomach. Beth had been acting a bit…odd the last few weeks. Yesterday at the final fitting for the bridal party dresses, she had burst into tears and had run from the room, muttering an apology afterward about wrong time of the month and always being a bridesmaid—or in this case maid of honor—and never a bride.

Michelle should have known Beth's reaction had to have been spurred by something more serious, but Michelle had been too wrapped up in her own wedding plans to give her best friend in the world the time she deserved. Now Beth was on her way over, and Michelle fought the miserable scenarios popping one after the other into her mind. Beth had been fired. Or transferred. She was sick. Needed a kidney. Or, *oh, Lord*, cancer. By the time the doorbell rang, she had her friend facing every catastrophe possible short of a tsunami.

"Go ahead and start dinner without me," Michelle called to her younger sister on her way down the hall. Yanking the front door open wide, she was startled to see her fiancé *and* her best friend. "Oh, Steven. I didn't expect your last-minute business to end so early. Why don't you go hang out with Corrie in the kitchen? She's eating supper. There's extra stroganoff on the stove. I'm just going to visit with Beth a little bit in the living room."

"Actually…" Steven stepped around Beth. "I brought Beth. We both need to talk to you."

"Oh. Well. All right." Adding confusion to the worry already simmering in her gut, she gave Beth a kiss on the cheek and Steven a quick peck on the lips.

Having been ushered out of the hallway and into the living room, after a moment of shuffling about, Beth and Steven took a seat on the sofa across from Michelle.

"Michelle—" Steven started.

"Let me," Beth interrupted.

"No. I think it will be easier if I explain."

"But this is my fault."

"This isn't a matter of fault." Steven moved his hand as if to reach out to Beth and quickly snatched it back. "Please."

Even more confused, Michelle watched the people closest to her in the world bickering, and wondered where exactly she fit into the conversation. "Somebody better tell me something, because neither of you are making any sense."

Eyes downcast, Beth nodded, and Steven took in a deep breath. "We've all been friends a long time."

"Yes. We have," Michelle agreed.

"Please." Steven held up his hand. "Just let me get through this."

Michelle inched forward on her seat and wondered what horrible scenario would include both Beth and Steven.

"As I was saying," Steven continued, "I met you and Beth at the same time. The three of us would go out together as often as you and I went out alone. The last few years, with all of Corrie's extracurricular activities conflicting with my social commitments, I think I've gone to more banquets and benefits with Beth than I did with you."

She twisted to face her long time friend. "And I can't thank you enough for stepping in for me so often with little notice."

Beth offered a weak nod.

"Well." Steven's gaze momentarily drifted away to the

fireplace and then settled back on Michelle. "You and I have been engaged for almost five years. This wedding has been delayed so many times, I don't think anyone in town expects us to actually get married. And quite frankly, I've been wondering for some time now if perhaps raising your little sister was just a handy excuse for not really wanting to marry me at all."

"That's not true." Michelle popped up from her seat and started toward Steven until he waved her back.

"Please. Sit." He waited an excruciatingly long moment while she retook her seat. "I'm only saying if we stop and look at the recent past, a long hard look, you'll agree. After all this time, I think we've both been in love with the idea of getting married rather than in love with each other. Not the way two people promising forever should be."

Michelle wanted to scream *you're wrong*, but her mouth wouldn't work. Of course she wanted to marry Steven. Who wouldn't want to marry someone as kind and generous and stable as him? Waiting for Steven to continue, she noticed Beth wringing her fingers, her eyes never lifting to meet Michelle's. Nothing was making sense.

And then it hit her. Steven was canceling the wedding and he'd brought Beth to hold her up. Keep her from falling apart. A role Beth had played well since childhood. A role that had been a lifesaver when Michelle's parents had died suddenly leaving her responsible for a ten-year-old little girl.

"You don't want to marry me," she whispered. The knot in her stomach twisted and snapped, doubling her over. All the time, the money, the dress—the guests.

"Sweetheart…Michelle, I know this is hard to face now, but in time I honestly believe you'll see the truth of what I'm saying. You don't really want to marry me."

Michelle lifted her head and looked at her now ex-fiancé. Only her gaze fell on his hand tightly entwined with Beth's. Beth had stopped fidgeting with her fingers and was now nibbling on her lower lip.

Michelle sat up straighter, taking a good look at her best friend. It couldn't be. When Beth glanced up and nodded,

Michelle almost lost her lunch.

"You?" Michelle managed to mumble.

This time Steven gave a silent nod. "Tomorrow morning we're leaving on the first flight to Vegas. Beth and I are getting married."

Whoever heard of a honeymoon for one?

"It makes perfect sense." Angie Cannon, a single, attractive brunette in her mid-thirties and Michelle's next-door neighbor for the last three years, stood with her hands on her hips staring at Michelle, as though she were completely daft.

"I..." What? Feel like a fool? Whether at sea or at home in Bluffview, feeling like a fool wasn't going to change anytime soon. So what could she say? "I can't leave Corrie home alone."

"I'll stay with her." Without hesitation, Angie volunteered to stand in for Michelle's missing former best friend.

Michelle shook her head. The original plan had been for Beth to stay with Michelle's sister, Corrie, while Michelle and Steven sailed the high seas. Of course with Beth and Steven honeymooning in Vegas, that left Michelle short not only one fiancé but also one best friend and teenage chaperone. "I can't ask you to do that."

"You're not asking, I'm offering. So pack your bags and go have a nice vacation."

Nice vacation? Ready to pull her hair from her head and run from the room screaming, Michelle was almost relieved at the sound of the Winchester door chimes. *Almost* being the key word. If she were really lucky, she'd find a pair of Jehovah's Witnesses on her front porch, but the way her luck had been running, it was more likely to be a modern day Typhoid Mary. Now wouldn't that solve all her problems?

Not bothering with the pretense of a smile, she swung

the door open and glared at whoever was on the other side.

"When you called in sick, I just knew something didn't feel right. Then I heard the news. I tried calling you." Pam Stuart from the office blew into the room like a gale force wind. "I got here as fast as I could. The nerve of the Back Stabber."

Ever since word had spread through town like proverbial wild fire about poor jilted Michelle, she'd been inundated with condolence calls over the death of her wedding. She'd finally taken the home phone off the hook and turned off her cell. So far, only her neighbor and coworker had been brave enough, or perhaps cared enough, to cross her threshold.

"Pam, this is my neighbor, Angie." Michelle waved toward the woman still standing in the middle of the living room with her hands fisted on her hips. "Pam and I work together at the newspaper."

The two women exchanged a brief smile along with *How do you do?* and *Nice to meet you.*

"Can I get you something to drink?" Michelle asked.

Pam shook her head. "No, thank you."

"Well, then." Angie took a seat on the sofa and turned to Michelle. "I repeat. You should go."

"Go where?" Pam asked, slowly descending onto the nearest chair.

"On the cruise," Angie answered Pam but kept her gaze on Michelle.

"On the *honeymoon* cruise," Michelle corrected.

A bright smile slowly bloomed on Pam's face. "Oh, I think that's a positively wonderful idea."

Was everyone in the room out of their ever loving minds except her? How could she explain to these people she didn't want to go on her honeymoon *alone*?

Pam jumped to her feet. "Think about it. You don't want to be here wallowing when the happy couple comes home."

Angie hissed in a breath, scrunching her face as though Pam's words had caused her physical pain.

Realizing what she'd said, Pam winced. "Sorry, honey.

You know I didn't mean that the way it sounded."

"I know. It's okay." But it wasn't okay. It would never be okay. Her perfectly planned wedding and *happily ever after* were shot to hell in a heartbeat. It had taken all day to cancel everything. The cake, the hall, the photographer, the caterer, the musicians. Thank heaven, Angie had taken over notifying all the guests.

The only thing left to cancel was the honeymoon. The cruise had been booked and paid for. Somewhere in the back of her mind, a small part of her agreed with Angie that it made sense to go ahead and take the trip. Unfortunately, for the better part of the day, the forefront of her mind had rejected good sense. A honeymoon for one could only add to the emptiness taking over her world.

Now Michelle stood in the middle of her living room, listening to both Pam and Angie plead their cases, and good sense seemed to be slowly gaining ground. After all, as Pam had not-so-subtly pointed out, the cruise would allow Michelle a brief escape from the forced smiles and pity-filled glances she would otherwise have to endure. Heaven knew she wanted to be in Bluffview when her ex-fiancé and her ex-best-friend/almost-maid-of-honor came back from their whirlwind Las Vegas wedding about as much as she wanted to suck on a bowl of sliced lemons.

"Okay, ladies. You win." Turning on her heel, Michelle marched up the stairs before she lost her courage. "If I'm leaving on a cruise, we'd better start packing."

Two hours later, Pam frowned down at the sleeveless cotton nightgown with pink ribbon edging as she handed it off to Michelle. "Honey, you should toss the granny jammies. What you need is to find yourself a gorgeous man or two and show them how to have fun. By the time you get back, well, it'll all be better. You'll see."

To Pam, fraternizing with the opposite sex was a recreational sport, which like baseball should be played nightly with an occasional doubleheader. Of course, that could explain how, at her age, Pam had already worn out four husbands.

All Michelle could manage was a curt nod and a meager

attempt at a smile that felt more like a nervous twitch.

Angie handed her the last piece of clothing to be packed. A one-piece navy blue bathing suit. A sensible, discreet design that somehow seemed to represent everything wrong with Michelle's life. Sensible, bland—and boring.

The next morning, all packed and ready to escape, Michelle rode with Angie, and Pam to the airport. Her newfound friends stood at security waving with broad grins on their faces. These two women, who a few days ago had been hardly more than a casual neighbor and coworker, now stood by her like a pair of two-by-fours holding up a crumbling roof. Any observers would never guess she'd been practically left at the altar and was off on her honeymoon alone.

Climbing over the ample aisle seat, she slid across to the window and cursed her ex-fiancé. Of course Steven—or as Pam had so adeptly named him, the Back Stabber—hadn't skimped. First-class seats. *I made the arrangements for the trip. You deserve the best. First class all the way.* Steven's words replayed in her head on a never-ending loop. Who was she kidding? There would be no escaping Steven Williams IV on this trip. Pam was right. Back Stabber.

"Would you care for some champagne before takeoff?" Holding a tray of little plastic champagne-filled glasses, the pretty blonde flight attendant smiled. Apparently, first class got to indulge in the bubbly while the rest of the passengers battled the bulging overhead compartments and squeezed into cramped seats unfit for anyone over the age of twelve.

"No thank..." She stopped midsentence. Why not? So what if Michelle Bradford only drank the bubbly on New Year's Eve? Did she really want to spend the next ten days sitting by, watching everyone else enjoy themselves? Pam was right. She deserved some fun. Champagne for breakfast. Caviar for lunch. Steak and lobster for dinner.

Michelle Bradford, prim and proper role model with granny jammies and sensible bathing suits, could just dang well stay in Bluffview. Michelle the swinging single had a lot of living to cram into ten days. Starting now.

CHAPTER TWO

"How the heck does anyone walk on these things?" Michelle mumbled, doing her best to strut down the hall. She knew full well her wobble looked more like a teenage boy in drag.

Once she'd made her decision to ditch her sensible side, she had realized there wouldn't be much swinging if she dressed like a small-town librarian. One of the flight attendants had suggested the best place to shop chic would be in South Miami Beach. Afraid she'd miss the ship's launch, she only had time to hit one store for her new wardrobe requirements. The perky little redhead at the boutique—who didn't look old enough to know the difference between Hollywood chic and bad taste—had assured Michelle she looked like an A-list star.

Now, the skimpy leather-strapped sandals pinched her feet, and the stiletto heels felt like she was balancing on toothpicks. But in the name of all the women left at the altar, she wasn't giving up. Finally, she conquered the distance from her stateroom to the ocean-view lounge. The round leather bar stools called to her like a siren's song. At least tomorrow, she could count on no one expecting her to wear strappy heels on the beach.

"What can I get you?" the bartender asked.

She slapped her cruise keycard on the counter and ignored the little angel on her shoulder pleading with her to order a diet cola. "Something exotic."

For a moment she thought the man was going to ask for more ID. The way he stared at her, one brow slightly higher than the other, he either thought she was too young, crazy, or maybe the salesgirl really did have bad taste. The eyebrow relaxed and he gave a curt bob of his chin. "One BBC for the lady."

BBC. That sounded much too much like British Broadcasting to be exotic. She glanced down at herself. Her bronze-colored backless sandal hung loosely from her foot. With her legs crossed, the short khaki skirt revealed a few more inches of thigh than she was comfortable with, still she resisted the urge to tug at the hem.

Let the real you show, the girl at the store had said. *You've got great legs. The world should know it*. Except with the thin fabric of her off-the-shoulder top and the ship's arctic air-conditioning puckering her nipples, she didn't doubt she was showing the world a lot more than just a little leg.

"Here you go." The bartender set the tall glass with a coconut slice and colorful umbrella in front of her. "Staying around for Name that Show?"

"For what?" Michelle's eyes remained fixed on the thick shakelike concoction. Her fingers reached forward, slowly, almost trembling. Oh, for heaven's sake, she scolded herself. It's not poison.

"Name that TV Show," he repeated. "It's a trivia game. One of the ship's entertainment crew will be gathering with passengers on the other side of the lounge by the grand piano." He pointed to a far corner of the large room. "It's fun. Good way to meet other passengers."

"Oh. Thank you." Holding the drink with both hands, she slid off the stool and took a fortifying sip before strutting, or wobbling, over to the other waiting passengers. "Hey, this is pretty good. What did you call it?"

"BBC. Baileys Banana Colada."

Forty minutes and three more BBCs later, with the cruise line cap her team had won in hand, Michelle sashayed into the casino. Apparently, all she needed to take the wobble out of her walk was a little Baileys.

"I play the nickel machines. There are only a few that still take coins, so I have to hurry to stake my claim." Sarah, one of her trivia teammates, pointed to her husband. "Big spender here likes the craps table."

"Absolutely." The man leaned over and kissed his wife briefly on the lips, and hurried off to the gaming tables across the crowded room.

Michelle shifted her weight and ignored the tug of jealousy that crept up at the easy marital gesture. "Well, the nickel slot machines sound more my speed, but I think I'll look around first."

"Sure. I'll probably still be here if you get bored." A plastic cup of coins gripped in one hand, Sarah slid onto a nearby seat.

The bustling sounds of slot machines dinging, roulette wheels spinning, and people chatting and cheering made Michelle want to play, too. For a few minutes she stopped and watched Sarah's husband at the craps table. People placed their chips on the felt table, and then one person would toss the dice. Chips moved back and forth, and every so often the table would burst out in a loud roar. Judging by the pile of chips at Sarah's husband's side, at least *he* knew what was going on.

When the waitress came by to take drink orders, Michelle hesitated. The sweet little angel on her shoulder was apoplectic over the four drinks she'd already had. But the little shopgirl whispering in her other ear convinced her that the concoctions were nothing more than glorified banana milkshakes. So she ordered another. Fresh drink in hand, she took a long sip and strolled over to the roulette table.

This she could do. With ten dollars of splurge money in her pocket, she wanted to play. Until now, she'd never realized how much of her life had been spent on the sidelines. Other people traveled on vacation, but not her, she saved her vacation time for spring-cleaning. Weekends were spent doing laundry and buying groceries. Jeez, venturing to the movie theater was about the biggest deal she had going. Especially since she usually waited for the movies to come out on DVD or stream. Cheaper that way.

But not now. For once, she would be part of the action. Setting down her half-empty drink, she handed the dealer her money and clutched at the round chips she received in return. What number to pick? The board behind the dealer showed all the recently winning numbers and colors. Nibbling on her lower lip, she studied the other players. A large older man stacked piles of chips on four or five different numbers. Next to him, a skinny brunette placed a short stack on black. The guy hanging over her shoulder picked twenty-one.

Everyone had placed their bets. The dealer spun the inner wheel in one direction and flicked the ball into play in the opposite direction. She was out of time. Had missed her chance. Then an arm reached out from behind her and set a short stack of chips on seventeen black. A deep voice rumbled, "Excuse me," and she dropped a chip.

In a desperate measure to cover her clumsiness, she slid the chip over to black. Safe bet, red or black. That should make the angel and the shopgirl battling inside her happy.

"No more bets."

She held her breath. Closed her eyes and then opened them in a flash. How stupid would she look standing at a roulette table with her eyes closed over a single chip bet?

"Black seventeen."

Her stare flung over to the man who'd sat beside her. His voice so low and sexy that two little words, *excuse me,* had her fumbling awkwardly. And no wonder. Everything about him screamed deep and sexy. Jet-black hair, Mediterranean-blue eyes, and a caramel-colored tan offset by a crisp white button-down shirt with the sleeves rolled up midway on strong forearms. Oh, yeah, definitely a player. The guy probably spent all his spare time sailing or on a tennis court. At a club. A private club. With a perky blonde on each arm.

Michelle moved a few inches away, took a sip of her BBC and set her winning chip down on black, again. The sexy arm reached forward and placed more chips on seventeen. Why would someone bet the same number twice? Surely the odds of winning were greatly decreased? She couldn't resist stealing a peek at him and almost fell over when she realized he'd been watching her. He winked. Their eyes had met, and he'd winked.

"No more bets."

She stared at the spinning wheel. She was not going to look at him. She wasn't.

"Black seventeen."

Okay, maybe one more time. He winked again, only this time he smiled, too. A big broad smile that showed gorgeous white teeth. Probably caps. But blast her knees felt wobbly again.

Not wanting to gawk like an awkward teenager, she smiled and snapped her attention back to the wheel. Time for a little change. One chip—oh, what the heck—two chips on red.

The sexy arm set a stack of chips on red sixteen but didn't move his hand away. Unable to resist, she stole a glance in his direction. His eyes watched her, almost as though he was waiting, but for what? She smiled thinly and turned her attention back to the wheel.

She had to stop looking at this man. His arm pulled away, and the dealer pushed the ball on the spinning wheel.

"No more bets." The whirling wheel slowed, the ball bounced, then stopped. "Red sixteen."

Mouth hanging open, her gaze flew to the stranger next to her. "How did you do that?" She hadn't meant to speak, but the words just tumbled out.

"I didn't. You did."

"Me?"

The waitress stepped up to take more orders. Mr. Sexy ordered bourbon on the rocks. Michelle ordered another BBC. The little angel on her shoulder must have gone to sleep because she wasn't warring with herself anymore. As a matter of fact…

"Maybe I'll try something different. What's that lady over there drinking?" Michelle pointed to the woman at the next roulette table holding a tall blue drink with skewered fruit perched on the rim.

"A Bahama Mama."

"I'll try that."

Michelle wasn't surprised to see the sexy stranger had returned his attention to the gaming table, but he hadn't yet placed his next bet. With both hands, he held a short stack of chips, lifting and dropping them back in his hand like an old Slinky.

In her hand she held four chips. Not a whopping amount of money. She'd already decided not to play the original ten dollars and only play with her winnings. Now the decision. Black or red? Her mom's birthday was November sixth. Both numbers black colors. She dropped a chip on black, and noticed Mr. Sexy on her left leaned forward and placed a bet on black twenty-four.

Sticking with black or red was a coward's bet. She was here to live and let live. Taking a deep breath, she leaned forward and placed a second chip on black eleven. "This is for you, Mama," she whispered softly.

Much to her surprise, Mr. Sexy moved his bet from twenty-four to eleven. Surely he wasn't following her lead? Oh, my. What if he was and she lost? Her chips were the lowest dollar amount available, but this guy's stack held the more expensive ones: ten…twenty…oh, good heavens, fifty dollars bet on her little old black eleven. Panic gripped her heart, strangling her breath.

"No more bets."

Her eyes squeezed closed. She didn't care who noticed. *Oh, pretty please.*

The croupier called, "Black eleven."

Her eyes sprang open, her jaw dropped, and her heart took off at a fast gallop. "We won?" Without thinking she whirled about and threw her arms around Mr. Sexy, then leaned back, squeaked, "We won!" and flung herself at him again.

"Yes, we did." His arms circled her waist, and his deep voice rumbled through her like an earthquake aftershock. "Want to do it again?"

CHAPTER THREE

avel's "Boléro" vibrated in Kirk's head. Every beat bounced off his bourbon-addled brain. Ignoring Ravel's obnoxious tune still blaring from his cell phone, Kirk buried his ears between two pillows, and cursed both Ravel and the moron at the bar who thought buying tequila shots for the fading crowd in the all-night disco was a good idea. Then he cursed himself for drinking them.

"Oh, all right." He threw the pillows across the small cabin and shuffled through his carry-on. "Hello!" Instantly, he regretted shouting into the phone. Someone had obviously used his head for an anvil. "Hello," he repeated more quietly.

"Wanted to see how you were making out flying solo this year," his friend Dave said.

"What time is it?" No matter how often he squeezed his eyes closed, then opened them, the numbers on his watch were still a blurry mess.

"Ten fifteen. I would have waited to check up on you, but Deb sent me to get something from the cafeteria, and I wasn't sure I'd get another chance to give you a quick call."

"Yeah, yeah. How's Deb's mom?"

"Not as bad as Deb had feared."

Kirk crawled back into bed and pulled the covers over his head. "I told you. It's just a broken hip. The way Deb carried on, you'd have thought it was a case of life or death."

"I know. But I'm not married to you. I can afford to tick you off. Besides, it's not like there aren't a flock of babes standing in line to keep you from getting lonesome. So what flavor was it last night? Blonde, redhead? What?"

Kirk pulled the phone away from his ear. He didn't remember his friend having such a loud voice. "Brunette." *I think.*

"Is she there now?" Dave lowered his voice to a whisper.

"Now?" Moving the covers down from his face and squinting at the light seeping through the partially opened drapes, Kirk glanced at the still made twin bed across the room. "No."

"Must be losing your touch."

"My touch is fine. We were closing down the place when some character started buying everyone tequila shots. Apparently, the lady doesn't hold her tequila well." That's right. She'd been feeling happy, but after the shots, neither one of them had been all that steady on their feet. "I deposited her safely in her room somewhere around five this morning."

"She must have really been sauced for you to go home alone."

"We both were. So if you don't mind, I'm going back to sleep until the sun goes down."

"No parasailing? I'm shocked."

"Oh, hell!" Kirk sprang from bed, and the floor shifted beneath him.

"What?"

He reached for his head, hoping to stop it from rolling off his shoulders. "I told…uh….um…what's-her-name we'd go parasailing. At least I think we agreed."

"You think? How much tequila did you drink?"

"Enough."

"Maybe she won't remember."

"Maybe, but if she does, I don't want to be a no-show. Tell Deb I'm glad her mom's okay, and that she owes me big time for letting you skip out on our annual trip."

"I'll let you tell her the last part. Have fun. And don't do anything I wouldn't do."

"If I do that, I might as well have stayed home." Kirk laughed, the throbbing in his head eased to a gentler pounding. What he needed was a long shower and a Bloody

Mary. Not necessarily in that order. Then he had to figure out where he'd agreed to meet…what's-her-name. "Talk to you when I get back."

"Great, man, and thanks again for understanding."

"No problem." Kirk tossed the phone onto the empty bed and rummaged through his bag for swim trunks. If he remembered correctly, and that was a very big *if*, he was supposed to meet… "What the heck is her name? Mary, Maddie, Megan, Mmmmiiichelle!" Right. Michelle. She'd seemed unsure about meeting him for breakfast and had finally agreed to meet him on the debarkation deck around eleven. If he hurried he might even have time to grab a little something fast to eat.

He hadn't quite figured the woman out. One minute she'd be dancing her heart out, hips swaying with moves that would make a pole dancer proud, and then she would turn all shy and demure, blushing like a virgin on her wedding night. Whatever the deal, he'd bet a week's salary she was a volcano ready to erupt, and he for sure planned to be there for the fireworks.

Ten fifty-five. Five more minutes and if he didn't show, Michelle would go back to bed where she belonged. Clutching her beach bag to her chest, she railed herself for leaving the luggage with her old clothes at the airport's baggage storage facility. Right now, she would give anything to have the boring, bland navy blue bathing suit back. This bikini barely hid what God gave her, and the cover-up had more holes than cover.

Ten fifty-six. What had she been thinking anyhow, agreeing to parasail? "Oh, sure I plan to parasail. Why come to the islands if you don't enjoy the water sports?"

Water sports. Flying through the air attached to a moving boat by a string wasn't sporting, it came closer to the definition of insanity. She should never have switched to the Bahama Mamas. She glanced at her wrist again. Ten fifty-seven.

Parasailing. *Steven Williams, this is all your fault. If you hadn't run off with my best friend, I'd be back in my cabin in bed where I belong!*

"Good morning."

That voice. Deep and low and sexy, the sound turned every ounce of her to molten *moosh*. "Morning. I, uh… I'm, uh, ready if you are."

"You bet. Never miss a chance to be out over the water, just me and the wind."

"You do this often then?" Keeping the beach bag in front of her like a shield, she handed the attendant by the open doorway her cabin card, and hoped Mr. Sexy couldn't hear her knees knocking. "I mean, come to the Caribbean?"

"I travel a lot with my job. Between assignments I like to take time to get away and have some real fun. Unwind."

Oh, yeah, she nodded mutely. Sure she knew. The last time she'd gone anywhere outside her small town was for her Gramma Betty's funeral in Boca Raton. Not exactly fun in the sun.

Not knowing what to say, she looked over the rail of the little boat taking them to shore. On the deck of the ship last night, she'd stood in awe of the low-hanging moon, shining a golden path across the shimmering black blanket of water. Now, looking at the water below in the light of day, she clamped her teeth together, not wanting to babble like the neophyte tourist she was. So many deep and glorious shades of blue, turquoise, and she supposed, this was the color God had in mind for aquamarine. She wanted to crawl over the side and swipe her hand through the crisp, clean water. "Isn't it gorgeous?"

"The water? Sure."

She stole a glance in his direction. "No wonder you like to come here to play."

Intently watching a colorful blue-and-green parasail off in the distance, Kirk lowered his eyes to meet hers and flashed a satisfied smile. "Work hard, play hard. Only way to stay sane."

What was it about this woman? Wisps of brown hair blew across her face. Delicate long fingers gripped the gear around her waist, occasionally breaking free to slip the delinquent strands of hair behind her ear. She still wore her swimsuit cover-up under the harness. When the attendant had suggested she would be more comfortable without it, she'd clutched at the front of the wrap like a shocked old Southern Baptist clutching her pearls, and then politely declined.

Kirk stepped into his harness, watching her fidget beside him from the corner of his eye. Her smile was big and cheerful, but her eyes held sheer terror. "You've never done this before, have you?"

"Not exactly."

Translation: not at all. Just what he thought. "You're gonna love it. There's nothing like it, flying in the air, free as a bird."

Her face momentarily blanched, and then he could almost see sheer will take over. Fearful eyes grew bright with enthusiasm, white-knuckled fingers loosened their hold on her harness, and the stiff broad smile now roared with laughter. "That's me. Free as a bird."

And she had been, for the rest of the day.

After parasailing, they'd stumbled off the speedboat giddy with laughter and high on adrenaline. She'd flung her cover off with the flair of a burlesque queen and handed him a bottle of lotion. "Would you mind? I can't reach."

Would he mind? Heavens, he'd been waiting since last night to get his hands on her. Slathering lotion across her silky skin was only the beginning of what he had in mind.

After that she'd become an unstoppable whirlwind. First, the paddleboats. Too tame. Then the kayaks. They'd spun around in circles a few times, which had them doubled over with laughter before they finally got the hang of rowing in unison. After a short break to refuel, she'd gone windsurfing. By the time they caught the last tender back to the ship, he was ready to drop. The woman flat wore him out.

Tilting her head to catch the sun, Michelle closed her eyes and took a deep breath as though trying to soak up every ounce of warmth possible. "I had a great time. Thanks for putting up with me."

"Back at ya." Kirk took advantage and looked at his new friend. Really looked. Smooth and curvaceous. Not in a balloonsized centerfold sort of way, but in that *the best things in life come in small packages* sort of way. Her bikini left little to the imagination, and his imagination already had the skimpy strings untied. He hoped she'd reapplied the sunblock often enough. It would be a real shame if his plans to turn his daydreams into reality had to take a backseat to second-degree sunburn.

The tender came to a stop, bobbing gently next to the ship. He stepped aside, letting Michelle lead the way. His gaze fixed on the sway of her hips. If all went well, tonight would definitely be the stuff dreams were made of.

What a day. Who'd have ever thought Michelle Bradford, Girl Scout troop leader, PTA secretary, and designated driver, would spend her day flying high with Mr. Sexy?

Clearly, the Miami salesgirl knew her stuff. Michelle looked, and felt, attractive and adventurous. Served the Back Stabber right.

Having opted for the gold backless minidress over the black sequined one with the plunging neckline, Michelle made every effort to tune out the annoying good angel whispering in her ear to tug on her skirt. The already short dress had shimmied up when she sat, looking dangerously close to…what was the word her sister used? Oh, yeah, *skanky*. But if the way Kirk kept sliding glances in her direction was any indication, the exhibition was well worth it.

"Would you like one?" the waiter asked, holding a tray

filled with colorful stemmed shot glasses.

"Are they all the same?" As if she would know the difference anyhow. Some of the glasses were red, some blue, and others green. They'd make great souvenirs. Maybe she could ask for an empty one?

Before she could open her mouth, the little shopgirl who'd spent the day arguing with the angel, once again whispered in her ear, "For heaven's sake. You're here to live and let live. You don't have to drive home. Pick one and drink it. Heck, drink 'em all."

All might be a bit much, but the voice was right. Adventurous women didn't ask for empty shot glasses. "I'll try the blue, please."

"One Italian Stallion."

Michelle felt the blush rise up her neck and settle in her cheeks.

Apparently, Kirk didn't have a low embarrassment threshold or a good angel on his shoulder. Not only had he ordered one of each for himself but he had the waiter set a red and green shot glass in front of her as well. *Oh, boy.*

Live and let live, she reminded herself. Plastering on a cheerful smile, she lifted the pretty blue glass, "Cheers!" and gulped it down in one swallow. "Mm. What did he say was in this?"

"Amaretto, Baileys, and Tia Maria."

"Ah, no wonder. I like Baileys."

Kirk took a small sip from his blue glass. "Baileys Banana Colada."

The fact he knew her preferred drink shouldn't have made a difference, but it did. She felt like a bubbling schoolgirl, effervescing with joy and ready to sing to the crowds, *Mr. Sexy noticed my favorite drink!*

She picked up the pretty red hourglass-shaped shot glass. "What's this one called?"

"French Kiss."

Didn't she wish! Good heavens, what was she thinking? The little shopgirl on her shoulder grinned knowingly. The overwhelmed angel cringed. Oh, yeah, the shopgirl definitely had the right idea.

"You should like that one, too." Kirk pointed with his chin at the glass in her hand.

"Baileys?"

He nodded.

This time she took a small sip. "You seem to know an awful lot about mixed drinks."

"Bartended to help pay for school."

"That sounds interesting."

He lifted his shoulder in a casual shrug, but somehow the gesture didn't seem casual at all. "It paid the bills."

The waiter appeared with their dinner, and she wondered if it had been the job, the money, or school in general that had posed a problem for her adventurous companion. "What did you study?"

"Business Administration." He cut into his steak, holding the morsel momentarily in midair. "This is one of the things I love about this line. They know what to do with their meats."

"Have you been on a lot of different cruise lines?"

He nodded and cut another piece. "All of them."

"All of them?" To keep her jaw from gaping open like a landed trout, Michelle shoved a forkful of salad into her mouth.

"Pretty much, yeah. I told you. Work hard, play hard."

"But how do you find the time to travel so much?"

"I'm self-employed. I take on a contract, and when it's over, I take off. *I* decide when it's time to work again. No one else."

"Surely, you must stay home once in a while? I mean, spend time with friends, family? Get the mail, do laundry, clean the house?" As much as she was enjoying herself playing the free spirit, she couldn't imagine being away from her sister all the time. For the last seven years, it had been just the two of them.

"Don't have any family. Most of my mail is just junk. I do all my banking and bill paying with my cell phone from anywhere in the world. As long as the housekeeper keeps the toilets clean I'm happy"—he shot her a lopsided grin—"and there's nothing to stop me from taking off for the next place on my list."

"Your list?"

"Right now I'm working on all the places in the song *Kokomo*."

"*Kokomo*? The Beach Boys' *Kokomo*?"

"Think about it. If you love the water, *Kokomo* is a great Caribbean guide. From Key Largo in Florida, to Montego Bay in Jamaica, Aruba, Bermuda, Bahamas. This trip I get to cross Martinique off my list. Next time I'm shooting for Montserrat."

"You mean there really is such a place?"

"Southeast of Puerto Rico. Half the island was buried under a volcano back in the nineties, so it's not a popular tourist place. But they say it's pristine in its beauty."

"And the friend who was supposed to take this trip with you, what was his name?"

"Dave."

"Right. Dave. Does he go off with you on all these adventures?"

"No, his wife would kill him." Kirk waved his steak knife in the air for emphasis. "After his first year of law school, his parents gave him an all-expenses-paid trip to Europe. That was the first time we took off together."

She stabbed at her salad. "Sounds expensive."

"Would have been, the way Dave's family had planned it out. Dave cashed in his business-class ticket for coach and dragged me along."

"Dragged you? To Europe?" She laughed out loud. "Like there's anyone in the world who wouldn't go running at an opportunity like that."

"Would you have?"

"Of course." Or maybe not. She'd dropped out of college to take a full-time job at the newspaper. The day her parents had died, she'd left frat parties, keggers, football games, and any girlish dreams behind. By the time her old friends were graduating, she'd built a busy new life raising her little sister and trying her best to fill her mom's shoes. There was no way she would have left Corrie to gallivant across the globe. They'd have had to drag her away from home kicking and screaming.

"Hey." Kirk waved a fork. "I lost you."

"Oh, sorry. My mind wandered."

"Am I that boring?"

"No. Not at all. Tell me more about the trip."

"It was great. Every kid grows up knowing there's more to the world than your own backyard. But it's different when you find yourself standing at the base of the Eiffel Tower, the foot of Buckingham Palace, or in the ruins of Pompeii. That's when I decided never to settle."

"Settle for what?"

"The ordinary. The bill of goods."

"Bill of goods?"

"I guess most people would call it the American dream. House with a picket fence, spouse, two-point-five children, and of course, a dog. A man who falls for that trap finds himself tied to a forty-hour-a-week job that turns into eighty so he can pay for the children, the house. And keep in mind, whatever time he's not working to pay for the house is spent fixing the house. I won't even get into what a wife costs a man."

"Ooh, a cynic."

"No, just practical. I don't want to wind up like an old rock-and-roll song."

"Rock-and-roll song?"

"You know. The one about the high school sweethearts whose life goes on even after the thrill of living is gone. I plan to enjoy the thrill of living until the day I die."

Kirk centered his knife and fork on the plate, and waved for the waiter.

A thin man, probably in his mid-fifties, the waiter scurried across the crowded floor. "Are you ready for dessert?"

The standard reply, *No, thank you. I don't eat sweets,* sprang to mind, but she managed to smother the words before they tumbled forth. "Anything with lots of chocolate."

The waiter turned to Kirk.

"I'll have the same, only with ice cream."

"Excellent." As quickly as he'd arrived, the waiter disappeared across the room.

"Where were we?" Kirk asked.

"The thrill of living. And your friend feels the same way?"

"He did until he fell into the trap."

"Ah, a house with two-point-five children?"

"A condo in San Francisco. No kids yet, but they've got the dog. I think Deb is letting Dave practice on the puppy before she entrusts him to fatherhood."

Now that made Michelle laugh. "But he still travels with you every year. Well, except this year."

"Deb's a good sport, for a wife. I get him two weeks a year, she gets him the other fifty, but enough on that. What will it be tonight? The casino? A show? Dancing?"

She didn't need an angel on her shoulder to know she should tell him *No, thank you.* After all, as a woman who looked both ways—twice—before crossing the street, she would have never wasted her time on a man who considered family a trap and believed playing hard the only way to live. That's why the last seven years of her life had been spent with Steven, a steady, responsible, respected citizen. Then again, look where that had gotten her.

In the two days spent with Kirk, she'd smiled, giggled, and laughed more than she had in the five years she'd been engaged to Steven. In eight more days she would be back to her regular routine in Bluffview. Responsible for a home, a teenager, and setting a good example. Her skirts would be long enough to cover her knees, her heels low and comfortable, her drinks nonalcoholic, and her life safe and sensible.

A monochromatic picture of her as an old woman sprang to mind. Rocking alone on the front porch, in a polyester polka- dot dress with sensible shoes, petting a sleeping cat. The poor old spinster left at the altar fifty years earlier.

By golly, if only for ten days of her long, sensible, and comfortable life, she would know the thrill of living. "I vote for dancing!"

CHAPTER FOUR

The morning sun winked at Michelle through the sliver of space between the drawn curtains. Snuggled comfortably in the warmth of her cabin, she burrowed deeper under the covers, and mumbled into her pillow, "Five more minutes."

"Mm," a baritone voice agreed as a heavy arm circled her middle and pulled her close against a strong hard body. The fuzzy patch of hair on his bare chest tickled the skin of her naked back.

Naked? Michelle's eyes flew open. The brazen sunlight shot painful daggers through her temple. She slammed her eyes shut, chasing away the shooting pain in her head, only to discover a simmering unease blooming in her gut.

Naked. She was naked…in bed…with a man. A naked man. Good grief, what had she done?

"Mornin'," the deep voice murmured in her ear.

"Mm," she mumbled back.

Vague memories slowly emerged from the recesses of her mind. Last night was all coming back to her. Kirk, the drinks, the laughter, the dancing. Oh, the dancing.

They'd done the two-step, the jive, an embarrassing rendition of the jitterbug, and a slow easy sway that couldn't truly be classified as dancing. With her cheek against his shoulder, and her body tucked against his, molded to him like a second skin, it wasn't any wonder they'd eased out of the disco, down the hall, and into the elevator without allowing an inch of space to grow between them. The moment the metallic doors closed behind them, his mouth had found hers. Heat on heat, the combustion had been instantaneous.

Entwined like a pair of tropical vines, they'd stumbled their way to her cabin. Once inside urgency had ruled. Buttons popped and fabric flew. Together they'd achieved pleasurable heights she hadn't believed possible. By the time they'd drifted off to sleep, she'd understood what her coworker Pam had been raving about all these years.

Now, heaven help her, she wanted to do it all over again. But the angel on her shoulder, shocked to find Michelle in bed with a virtual stranger, chastised her for being so reckless. The voice of reason urged her to find her clothes, pack her bags, get off at the next port, escape temptation, and return as fast as she could to her orderly sensible life.

Just as reason began to take hold, as duty pushed passed desire, Kirk's warm mouth nibbled on her neck, sending shivers down her very tense spine.

"Delicious. Micki mine," he whispered against her skin.

Oh, yeah. His sweet lips worked a path of nerve-tingling kisses down her neck and across her shoulder.

Like the tide pulled by the moon, her body shifted, turned in his arms.

To hell with reason.

Maybe she'd gone too far this time. Her legs ached, and if she shifted the wrong way, she would get the mother of all wedgies, again.

Why did people think this was fun? Every touch was like gripping paint-covered sandpaper, not really smooth, not really rough. All for what? To reach the heights and ring the dang bell.

When Michelle saw one of the rock climbers get a shock from touching the metal screws on the next grip and come sliding back down, she almost handed over her harness and walked away. Then a kid half her size rang the bell, glided to the bottom, landed with a spring to his step, and her fears seemed grossly out of place.

Now, halfway up the wall, she was rethinking her strategy. Would she really look that foolish if she just gave up and slid down? Then again, if what goes up must come down, she might as well come down from the top. It was that kind of crazy thinking that had gotten her here in the first place, letting the idea of Micki Bradford, adventurous fun-loving woman, get the better of her. No matter what nickname Kirk called her by, deep inside she was still boring, sensible Michelle. A woman who had to be out of her mind to climb halfway up a fake mountain.

One step at a time. She blew out a resigned breath and pushed with her legs. She could do this. Fighting the urge to look down, she reached for the next groove in the wall and the next. Eyes upward, the insurmountable distance to the top had shrunk to just one more reach. Stretching, careful not to swing away from the wall, arm extended, she pulled on the string.

The bell clanged and something inside her soared. She'd done it! She'd actually done it. She'd climbed a forty-foot wall. Conquered the wedgies, the sore fingers, the tired legs, and rung the bell. Careful not to touch the rope on the ride down, she landed on her feet and gleefully spun around to find Kirk.

"Race you to the top!"

There was an excitement about Micki that Kirk couldn't ignore. A contagious energy. With her the same old, same old, seemed fresh and new. Again today, at the last port of call, walking the crowded tourist market, a place like every other open-air market on every other island he'd ever been, he was sucked in by her enthusiasm, searching for the next great bargain.

"How much is this?" She wore a floppy hat, a thin green strand of straw delicately woven along the brim.

"For you, pretty lady, only twenty-five dollars."

Kirk swallowed the urge to laugh out loud. This poor

island woman had no idea what she was in for. His Micki might look like an ordinary tourist but lurking inside was a shrewd woman who could put the Donald's famed negotiating skills to shame. Kirk had been watching her all morning. If she wanted that hat, and he'd come to recognize the glint in her eye when she found something she absolutely wanted, she would get it and *not* for twenty-five dollars.

"Thank you, no." She bit back a smile and handed over the hat. She'd done this on every island port. She either had a family the size of the Osmonds or enough friends to fill a town. Either way, he loved watching her shop, seek out the perfect gift for a loved one, and then haggle her way to a fair price.

"This is handmade, not machine made. Normally I sell these for thirty dollars. Today you can have it for only twenty."

"Ten."

"No, miss. Look at the quality. Eighteen."

Micki shook her head, and took only one step before the woman countered, "Fifteen."

"Ten," Micki repeated. She'd found a similar hat for that price earlier that she wasn't as fond of and had apparently decided that would be a fair price.

The woman hesitated a second. "Twelve. I can do no better than that."

"Thank you, but I'm not willing to pay more than ten." On that, she turned on her heel, had taken two steps when the woman shoved the hat in her hand.

"Ten dollars for the pretty miss."

It was all he could do to stop himself from kissing the big grin off her face. If he told Dave how much fun he'd had walking every aisle of the crowded tourist market, his friend would have him undergoing a full medical exam, maybe even psychiatric testing.

For the umpteenth time today, Kirk had almost broken his steadfast rule and asked Micki for her phone number. So far, she'd been the perfect shipboard companion. Together, they'd laughed hard and played hard. Nothing existed outside the here and now. She knew the rules of the game as well as he did.

With the exception of their dinner the first evening of the cruise where he'd talked about his trip with Dave that launched his love of travel, neither had divulged anything personal. For all he knew, she had a husband and two-point-five children at home waiting for her. Though he doubted it.

So many times over the last nine days he'd wondered, What was her story? Why was she here on a ship alone? For most women traveling solitaire, the answer was easy—men and sex. Except from day one, he knew this intriguing lady was different. Still, he'd held fast to the unspoken rules of a shipboard liaison—don't ask, don't tell.

Besides, he also knew, back in the real world, there was no such thing as different. All women were the same. The American dream was nothing more than a well-marketed trap, and he wanted no part of it. Next trip there'd be another woman to liaise with. There'd always be more women, but he knew they'd be like all the women before Micki. Same old, same old.

Stopping short in front of him, that now familiar twinkle gleaming in her eye, she seemed to have zeroed in on one of the gold charms in the jeweler's window.

"Shall we go inside?" he asked. The question must have been more difficult than he realized. She nibbled on her bottom lip as though debating the solution to world peace. "Micki?"

"Um, sure."

A middle-aged man with a slight British accent in a crisp white suit approached. "May I help you?"

She pointed to the front of the store. "I'd like to see the charm in the window. The bird flying."

"Certainly."

Her eyes followed the man as he moved to unlock the window and returned with the large gold charm, then set it on a black velvet board in front of them. "This is a lovely piece."

"Mm," she agreed.

Wings spread wide in flight, the bird, probably a

seagull, appeared to be soaring upward. His head, in profile, had a single eye. A tiny deep green emerald, shining brightly. The piece was absolutely beautiful.

Timid fingers made a casual attempt to flip the tag. The sparkle of longing in her eyes was eclipsed by sticker shock. Most likely a one-of-a-kind piece, the charm was priced accordingly.

"This is eighteen karat gold. Though small, the emerald is high quality from Colombia."

"Yes. Thank you." Micki smiled and stepped back.

"We'll take it." Kirk hadn't noticed if she'd worn any jewelry on the ship. She would need a necklace or bracelet to wear the charm on. A bracelet. Somehow he knew a discreet bracelet was something she would be more likely to wear back home. "And a bracelet, too."

"Oh, no." Eyes wide with surprise, her hand reached over and covered his. "I can't let you do that. It's lovely, but—"

"Work hard, play hard." He turned his hand under hers, linked fingers, and offered a gentle squeeze. "This is our last day. I'd like you to have it."

For a few long seconds he noticed something in her gaze he hadn't seen before—sorrow. He'd wanted the gift to make her happy not sad. And then, as if it had been nothing more than his imagination, the delightful twinkle in her eyes returned.

"Thank you." Her hold on their clasped hands tightened. "I'd like that, too."

CHAPTER FIVE

"I can't get over it. You look fabulous!" Angie, Michelle's neighbor, helped carry the luggage upstairs to her room.

"I gotta admit," Corrie chimed in, "you really do look hot in that outfit."

"Mm." Michelle had barely had enough time to retrieve her old luggage and check in for her flight, never mind change into her old clothes. It nearly killed her to pay the airline's extra baggage fees for all the cruise clothes she would probably never wear again in her life. But she wasn't leaving them behind, either. Maybe she could donate them to a woman's shelter or something.

Right. Like women's shelters really need cruise clothes, especially the cocktail dresses. She could probably store the clothes-filled suitcases in the attic. Maybe someday she'd take another trip. Maybe even with Kirk. *Right*. She didn't know a dang thing about him other than his first name and that he had a cute little heart-shaped birthmark on his left hip. Like she could put that data into a search engine to locate him. She had no idea where he called home or what he did for a living. All she'd learned was Kirk did consulting. Whatever that meant. For all she knew, he could be a Mafia hit man.

She glanced around the room and noted, for the first time, all the shades of beige. Not a single bright color to liven things up. This was her reality. The trip was over. *The thrill of living* and *free as a bird* were history. Home less than two hours and already she wondered if any of it had been real. Her left hand closed over the dangling charm on her right wrist. *Definitely real.*

Corrie plopped onto her sister's bed. "Steven has called every day since their return from Vegas. I saved all the messages."

Angie pressed her lips together and glared at the kid. Pam rolled her eyes and gently brushed Michelle's arm. "We weren't going to mention *him* yet. Give you some time to settle in first.

"It's not like she can avoid them forever," Corrie continued. "I mean, Beth's her best friend."

"Was," Pam snapped.

"Is, was, whatever." Corrie waved a dismissive gesture. "Do you know they've been home almost a week, and Beth has hardly left the house. I heard she took a leave of absence from work."

"How could your sister know? She's been away having a great time without the Back Stabber. Haven't ya, hon?"

"Pam, please."

Pam huffed out a frustrated sigh. "Oh, for land sakes. Corrie's not a baby."

"'Bout time someone noticed." Corrie folded her arms across her chest, and bobbed her head to emphasize her point.

Before turning back to Michelle, Pam shot the teenager a don't-push-your-luck glare. "Tell us about the trip. I'm guessing from that nice tan you've got that you didn't spend the whole time locked up in your cabin."

Not the whole time. Michelle bit back the smile that threatened to overtake her face, slid the now empty suitcase under her bed, then opened the bag with all the gifts she'd bought. On top was the pink-and-white Prada knockoff purse she'd nabbed in Nassau for only ten dollars.

Corrie leaped from her corner of the bed to snatch it up. "Sweet."

"Good, because it's for you." At the time Michelle had debated between the small pink or the larger brown. Until now she hadn't been sure she'd made the right choice. "I, uh, gather Beth moved into Steven's house?" she said softly, sifting through more items.

"So we *are* gonna talk about this?" Pam sank into a

nearby chair.

"No." Michelle kicked off the stiletto heels she'd grown accustomed to walking in and slipped on her Bugs Bunny slippers. For at least a little while longer she was going to wallow in the wake of the best ten days of her life. She handed Pam a set of brightly painted wooden fish. "Here."

Pam scooped up the multisized fishes. "I love them!"

"The moment I saw them, I knew they were meant for you." Michelle turned to Angie and handed her a heavy bundle of towels.

"What's this?"

"You gift. Well, inside all the padding is your gift. I didn't want it to break."

Balancing the bundle on her lap, Angie slowly removed the layers of beach towels. "Oh, my!"

"To add to your collection." Michelle wasn't sure if the Caribbean theme might be too over-the-top for Angie's more traditional teapot collection. If she'd been shopping for Beth, Michelle wouldn't have had any trouble picking the perfect gift. She knew Beth Norton better than she knew herself. Or so she'd thought.

"It's lovely." Angie held up the small teapot. Designed to look like an island cottage, the lid doubled as the tan thatched roof, the square base consisted of a sky-blue house with pink windows, and splashes of yellow, purple, and red flowers. Trunks of palm trees on either side formed the spout and handle. Her smile beamed. "Wow. This is beautiful. So different from anything else I have. Thank you."

"No, thank you for convincing me to go and for staying with my sister."

She'd bought some more stuff for her sister, a T-shirt that changed colors in the sun, flip-flops covered in tiny seashells, and a myriad of other gewgaws she couldn't resist splurging on.

"What's this?" Corrie placed the straw hat on her head, laughing. "Like you'll have anywhere in Bluffview you could wear this."

"That's enough, young lady." Michelle reached out to

retrieve her hat when Pam's fingers wrapped around her wrist.

"Never mind the hat. *What* is *this*?"

"I believe it's called a charm bracelet," She said the words with as much aplomb as she could muster.

Pam studied the piece more carefully, stealing a glance in Michelle's direction before looking back again. "This, my friend, is not the sort of thing a woman usually buys for herself. Spill."

"There's nothing to *spill*. I don't usually take vacations or go parasailing, but I did. I saw this in the store window and fell in love with it. That's all." And that was all. The fact that she didn't buy it for herself was irrelevant.

Corrie sprang to her knees, her eyes round as the moon. "You went parasailing?"

"I did." She hadn't meant to let that slip, but at least Pam was off the scent of the bracelet.

"Really?" Angie asked.

"Really." Zipping the suitcase shut, Michelle brushed her hands together and looked to her friends and sister, a waiting audience expecting more information. Too bad she wasn't planning on sharing anything else. Adventurous Micki was gone. Steadfast Michelle was back. "So, what's for dinner?"

"Hey, man." Kirk followed his friend Dave over to the baggage claim. "I didn't expect to see you here."

"Deb and I agreed picking you up at the airport and feeding you dinner was the least we could do after I crapped out on you at the last minute."

Kirk lifted a lazy shoulder. "It all worked out."

"How'd things go with the brunette? She was a brunette?"

"Yeah. And okay." He didn't know why, but he didn't feel like talking about Micki.

"That bad?"

Kirk spotted his bag and pulled it off the carousel. "It was fine. You know how cruises are. They're pretty much all the same. Seen one island, you've seen them all."

"Right. How was Martinique?"

"Wet. It's a rain forest." Apparently he didn't feel much like talking about any of the trip.

"Next trip is where? Montserrat, right?"

"Unless I land the Cairo contract. If that comes through, Montserrat will have to wait."

Dave led the way to the parking lot. "You think you have a chance at it?"

"Not really, but it would be one helluva break. Global reputation, playing with the big boys."

"And in the meantime?"

"I've got a small sweeper contract for the communications group I did the radio station job for a couple of years ago. Now they're into buying and dismantling newspapers. Project starts Monday."

"That soon. How long you figure it'll take?"

"Short and sweet. Preliminary info seems pretty cut and dry. Small-town operation, excess spending, overstaffed, stuck on doing things the way they've always been done. I should be in and out in less than six weeks. Eight tops. If Cairo calls, I'll be ready to rock and roll."

Dave clicked the key fob unlocking his car doors from several car lengths away. "Don't you ever get tired of playing Ebenezer Scrooge? Always looking at the bottom line?"

"That's what I get paid for. And very well might add. You can't take a company from the red to black if you ignore the bottom line."

"Right." Dave popped open the trunk and waited for Kirk to load his suitcase before slamming it shut. "Listen, Deb's waiting for us at the apartment. You don't mind if we eat in, do you?"

Kirk slid into the car and buckled his seat belt. "Depends on whether or not she's taking another cooking class and plans to use me as a guinea pig."

"No." Dave smiled. "Her brief foray into Chinese

delicacies was her last. From now on it's strictly down-home cooking. I'm hoping to prove a terrace is all the outdoor entertaining space we need."

"Ah, she's in buy-a-house mode now, isn't she?"

Dave pulled out of the parking lot. "Don't start on me."

"I warned you, man. In the beginning they're all sweet and agreeable. Then everything goes to Hades in a hand basket. First, it was the dog, now it's the house. Next it's the kids, then the bigger house, the college fund, and the club sports team. You'll be locked in an office sixteen to twenty hours a day, six to seven days a week to pay for all of it. Twenty years down the road, while you're working your butt off to pay for your family's lifestyle, that sweet young girl you married runs off with another guy 'cause you don't have time to have fun like you used to. The American trap. A slow, steady decline."

Dave shook his head. "Someday, buddy, you're going to meet a woman who shoots all that cynicism to hell, and I plan on having a front-row seat when she does."

"Won't ever happen." In twelve years, only one woman ever made him rethink his set-in-stone rule of no strings attached. In the end, he'd resisted the temptation. No, he was safe. He doubted he would ever run into another Micki Bradford in his lifetime. "So, what's for dinner?"

So far, so good. Almost an entire day home in her real world, and Michelle was holding up just fine. With Angie, and Corrie, she sat nestled in a back booth at The Pancake House just outside the city limits. Pam offered to break her date with Bernie Crawford to join them, but Michelle insisted it wasn't necessary.

After ten days of nonstop gourmet meals, even though it was suppertime, all she craved was a tall order of blueberry whole wheat pancakes with low calorie syrup. Besides, she wasn't ready to face a world with her best friend and fiancé married to each other. Not yet, and anyplace in town she was bound to run into someone who wanted to gab about the newlyweds. Or worse, bump into the newlyweds themselves. The Pancake House was just far enough away to assure her a peaceful dinner in a Steven-and-Beth-free zone.

"Did I miss anything important while I was gone?" she asked.

Angie developed a sudden interest in the silverware, and Corrie focused much too intently on sipping her soda.

"Okay. What happened?"

Corrie pushed the drink away and leaned back in her seat. "You might as well tell her."

"No. We agreed. *You* did it. *You* tell her."

"It's no big deal really. Just a little party."

Angie began tapping her forefinger on the table.

"All right. I told Angie I was spending the night at Brittany's. Brittany told her mom she'd be spending the night at our house."

Probably the oldest trick in the teenager handbook, but Michelle never thought she would have to worry about her little sister pulling that stunt on her or on the person she'd left in charge for ten days. "Go on."

Corrie stared into her drink, twirling the straw. "You remember the Sadie's dance was the Saturday after you left."

Michelle nodded.

"Billy Webb hosted the after party. An all-night party."

Michelle never hid her feelings well, and her shock must have showed, because when Corrie looked up from her drink, she rambled on more quickly.

"It's not like his folks weren't there or anything. And it was a small party. His mom said he could have twenty people. I knew you wouldn't let me go, so I didn't ask. But after you left, we figured out Angie would let me stay at Brittany's, and if Brittany's mom thought she was here, well…" Corrie shrugged.

"Just tell me what happened."

"Angie called Brittany's house to check on us—"

"Actually, I called to find out what time you wanted me

to pick you up," Angie interrupted. "Not the same thing."

"I'd told you I didn't need a ride home." Corrie was whining much like she had as a child in the grocery cart after their mom had said no to all the candy in the check out lane.

"I know, but you didn't take the car, and I didn't want Brittany's mom to think she had to bring you home. Besides, I didn't know if her family had plans for the next day, and I didn't want to disrupt them."

So far it sounded like exactly what Michelle would have done.

"We'd only been at Billy's for about an hour," Corrie continued, "when Angie and Brittany's mom showed up to drag us home. It was *so* embarrassing."

"She's been grounded for almost a week." Angie pushed her plate away. "She's all yours now."

Michelle stared at her little sister. What would her mother have done? Said? At least Corrie had the good graces to look repentant, but was that an act? She couldn't take a chance. Couldn't risk Corrie making any more mistakes. "And so are the car keys."

Corrie's gaze met hers. "The car?"

Michelle nodded, expecting an argument or a tearful plea. Instead, like a set of matching bookends, Corrie and Angie turned stiff as stone. Their faces ashen. Like matching bookends their gazes glazed over, locked on the same distant point. And then Michelle knew. She didn't have to turn around to see, she just knew. "Are they coming this way?"

Angie slid her gaze to Michelle. "I don't think they see us."

"No." Corrie relaxed. "They've gone the other way. Around the corner."

Palms sweating, Michelle rubbed her hands along the sides her jeans. "It's okay. I'm bound to bump into them sometime." Of course it was inevitable that she would run in to her ex-fiancé and his new bride around town eventually. Bluffview wasn't a major metropolis. She couldn't hide forever. Still, she hadn't expected to run into them here. Tonight. Her heart raced at warp speed, and her stomach flipped over, then sank to the floor. *I'm not ready. Not yet. Not now.*

"I'll get the check." Angie waved at the waitress behind the counter, Michelle nodded.

The next few minutes passed in a silent haze. Whatever Angie and Corrie might have said, Michelle didn't hear them. All she wanted was to get out of the restaurant unseen by Steven and Beth. And she wasn't even going to think about seeing *them.* There wasn't enough time in the day to prepare herself for a glimpse of the happy newlyweds. Walking closely behind Angie, she kept her eyes on the exit. Almost afraid to breathe as if that might make her more noticeable.

Out the door, she took a deep breath and stopped herself from running across the parking lot. Fueled by the urge to flee, she beat Angie and Corrie to the car by several paces. Buckled in the front seat, she told herself not to look.

Fingers curled around the steering wheel, she pulled out of the space and pointed the car toward the exit. Eyes focused on the ground ahead, she would not look. She wouldn't. But she did.

In the booth by the window she saw them. Holding hands. Michelle's grip on the steering wheel tightened, her knuckles grew white with tension. Only weeks ago she'd been the one trying to eat with just one hand while Steven held the other. They had been the couple anticipating a happy life, imagining growing old together. She tried to look away. Ignore the hurt. She wanted to hurry home and hide in the safety of her bedroom, to forget the betrayal.

Instead, the car slowed and her gaze locked on Beth. Her best friend since kindergarten straightened her shoulders, pulled her hand back, then turned to look out the window.

"Michelle?"

Despite the concern in her sister's voice, Michelle couldn't turn away, couldn't stop looking, wondering. How? Why? Foot firmly on the brake, her gaze lingered until Beth's gaze latched onto hers.

"Shouldn't we be going?" Angie asked, her voice dripping with the same concern as Corrie's.

"Yes. Yes, we should." Michelle dragged her gaze away, stepped on the gas, and turned the car toward the street. Everything was all wrong.

CHAPTER SIX

onday couldn't have come fast enough. A house had only so much dust, and two people just didn't generate that much dirty laundry. If Michelle had scrubbed her bathroom one more time, she'd have stripped the glaze clean off and turned the ceramic tile to dust.

At the office, stacks of files teetered precariously on her normally orderly desk. At least now she had something to keep her mind busy, distracted. It would take her weeks to catch up. *Thank heaven.*

Maybe if she buried herself in paperwork, she wouldn't notice how every person who passed by her desk looked at her as though she'd lost her best friend. Both of them.

"Want to talk?" Pam leaned against the file-laden desk.

"It's not as bad as it looks. I should be able to find my desktop in a decade or so."

"That's not what I meant, and you know it."

Yeah, she knew, except she'd spent all morning trying to forget that her fiancé and best friend were now husband and wife.

"Okay, I'll play along." Pam dropped a manila file on Michelle's desk. "We've got the final numbers on last quarter."

Michelle moved the pencil holder Pam had bumped an inch back to its proper place, then opened the file and leafed through the pages. "Ooh," she hissed. "This is worse than I thought."

Pam nodded. Each page was bleaker than the one before. Ad revenues were falling like stones off a cliff.

"There's more."

Michelle closed the folder, tapped it on her desk and set

it squarely on the short stack of files she'd been working with. "Do I really want to know?"

"Depends on how much you like your job."

"About as much as I like to eat."

"While you were away, we got the word. Mr. Harrison is gone. They're sending some new hotshot hatchet man to trim the fat."

"Oh, my. Ed Harrison has been here since—"

"Forever," Pam finished for her.

Michelle's stomach did a nervous flip. "How many jobs will be cut?"

"Sally from personnel didn't say. Supposedly Mr. Hatchet Man is only coming to *evaluate*, but we all know what that really means."

"Blast. I'd hoped some of the new sales incentives would help the numbers. When is this new guy expected to arrive?"

"Sometime today."

Michelle swallowed her surprise, set the pen on her desk and leaned back in her chair. Hopefully she'd struck a casual, laissez-faire pose, but she was pretty sure her body language screamed *jilted bride in denial.* "Do we know anything more about him? Like for starters, his name?"

Pam nodded and crossed her ankles. "Lloyd McEntire."

"Lloyd? What kind of a name is that? No one names their kid Lloyd anymore. The man must be older than my aunt Millie's heirlooms."

"All I know is he's supposed to be some kind of miracle worker. The Lee Iacocca of the new millennium. Sally says he's the guy responsible for turning around Stereo City."

"What's a guy who not only saves a regional retail outlet from bankruptcy but turns it into the number one national electronics store doing tinkering with a newspaper?"

Pam shrugged. "Beats me. But last week, Harmon Brody came down from corporate to make sure we had everything up to speed before Mr. Hatchet Ma...I mean McEntire gets here. You remember Harmon, don't ya?"

"Wasn't he the skinny fellow who always wore bow ties?"

"That's him. He's done real well for himself at headquarters. We went out for a few drinks. Not till his last day in Bluffview, of course. You know, appearances and all."

Michelle almost laughed. Since when did the flaming redhead dressed in bright purple care about appearances?

"Anyhow, when I had him good and buttered up"—Pam looked around, and leaned closer—"he told me McEntire's our last hope. We've been bleeding red ink for so long, some of the higher-ups are just itching to board us up and write us off."

A small hammer started banging between Michelle's eyes. "This McEntire better be a sanctified miracle worker. I can't afford to lose this job. I can't."

"None of us can, honey. But don't you worry. I've done a little checking around, and this guy is *the* best. Really he is."

"Excuse me." A male voice came from behind Michelle. A deep, sexy, and dear-Lord-it-couldn't-be familiar voice. "I was told I'd find Mr. Harrison's assistant here."

Pam straightened to her full height, puffing her chest out and grinning like a cat about to pounce on her next canary. "I'm Pamela Stuart. How may I help you?"

Michelle held her breath. It couldn't be him. Kirk most likely lived somewhere in California. Probably scoping out his next Mafia hit at this very moment. Or jumping out of an airplane somewhere.

"I'm Lloyd McEntire. I'll be replacing Mr. Harrison temporarily."

She breathed a relieved sigh. But how could two men have that same bone-melting silky voice? And how the heck was she supposed to work with someone whose every word would remind her of the ten best days of her life? She had no idea, but sitting with her back to her new boss was most definitely not the smartest way to keep her job.

Rolling her chair to the side, she pushed to her feet and turned to meet… "Holy Moses."

Michelle looked about to keel over. All color drained from her face, and if Pam wasn't mistaken, her friend had just mumbled, *Holy Moses.*

Thinking maybe the Back Stabber had summoned the courage to come into the office, Pam glanced around Mr. McEntire. Except for the new receptionist coming down the hall with a cup of coffee, the place was deserted.

Beside Pam, with eyes round as dinner plates, Michelle stared openmouthed at their new boss. Granted the guy was handsome as the devil and tempting as sin, but that was no reason for Michelle to be teetering in place like a woman who had just drunk her lunch straight from a bottle in a brown paper bag.

And if the deep crease embedded between Mr. McEntire's brows was any indication, the man appeared to be as confused as Pam by Michelle's odd behavior. "This is Michelle Bradford," Pam said, "local ad manager."

His brows lifted, and Pam thought she saw a hint of a smile tug at one side of his mouth. "Micki—"

"Nice to meet you," Michelle blurted quickly, cutting him off and sticking her hand out so fast she almost stabbed the man in the midsection.

Dark brows knitted together briefly before his expression cleared to a blank slate. "Nice to meet you, too."

"If you'll excuse me." Michelle stepped to the side, tripping over her chair. "I have some things to take care of." Backing up a step, she pointed at Pam. "You'll be in good hands. Um, I mean, Pam will take good care of you." She stepped back again and took a deep breath. "That is, Pam will show you around. I mean, your office. Won't you, Pam?"

Pam nodded at her friend who'd managed to stumble backward halfway down the hall, then Pam smiled stiffly at the handsome hunk in front of her. "Right this way, sir."

Without a single glance back in Michelle's direction, Lloyd McEntire followed the sassy redhead. The moment the large wooden door—of what had until recently been Mr. Harrison's office—clicked shut, Michelle spun around, ran to the ladies' room and didn't stop until she stood in a stall, her back pressed to the bolted door. "Oh, my."

Clutching her stomach as though she'd been punched—hard—she took in a long deep breath and blew it out very slowly. The last thing she needed was to hyperventilate. Hiding in the bathroom like a melodramatic teenager was bad enough. Someone finding her passed out by the toilet would be beyond mortifying.

She drew another slow deep breath and then another. The mind-numbing shock had begun to ease, but her legs were none too steady. Shifting around in the small space, she closed the toilet lid and sat. "Of all the gin joints."

Lloyd McEntire. He'd lied. Given her a fake name. She almost laughed. How pathetic she must have seemed to him. On the cruise it hadn't taken long for her to understand, other than the few tidbits about his college days, Kirk wouldn't talk about his life off the ship. For him there seemed to be only the then and there. And frankly, at the time the idea of making the outside world off-limits suited her fine. She didn't want to be pitied. The jilted bride. Yes, at the time it all made sense. A cruise fling. No ties to the life on land, just fun in the sun. But to not give her his real name?

Elbows on her knees, she dropped her head into the palms of her hands. At least she'd stopped him from giving her away. When he'd used his nickname for her, her heart almost stopped.

He was supposed to be her private little memory. Tucked away in the back of her mind to be brought out and dusted off every decade or so. He wasn't supposed to show up in her town. At her job. As her boss, temporary or otherwise. "Blast."

No one could find out. How would she explain him, *the two of them*, to her young impressionable sister? Taking another deep breath, she straightened her spine. She wouldn't have to explain. No one would have to know. He hadn't given her away. Surely that meant he would be willing to ignore their recent…history?

Of course. The nervous flutter in her stomach slowed. Just because he was here didn't mean he wanted to pick up where they'd left off. There was no reason they couldn't function in the same office and maintain a reasonable working relationship. After all, she hardly ever dealt with Mr. Harrison. If she kept to herself, burying her head in paperwork, she might not have to see *him* much at all.

Standing up, her legs felt stronger, her stomach more settled, and her breathing easier. She could do this. Everything would be fine. She'd do her job. Keep to herself. Yeah. Everything would be fine.

"Michelle, you in here?" Pam's voice drifted over the stall.

She unlocked the door and swung it open. "Yes."

"You okay, honey?"

Still shaky fingers brushed at the sides of her skirt, smoothing away nonexistent wrinkles. She nodded.

"Then what in the name of all that is holy has gotten into you? I've never seen you act so scatterbrained."

"Nothing." She flashed a brief smile. "Everything's fine."

Pam raised her hands to her hips, tipped her head, and glared at Michelle with the searing precision of X-ray vision. "You're not telling me something."

"I promise you, I'm okay. I just felt a little queasy and needed to get to the rest room." That much was the truth. "Probably some bad leftovers. I'll have to clean out the fridge when I get home." One little white lie wouldn't hurt anyone. Besides, Pam had no way of knowing Michelle had already scrubbed the refrigerator and every other appliance in her kitchen to within an inch of its metallic life.

"Okay. But whatever you do, don't throw up on the new guy. Our jobs may depend on it."

Michelle splashed a little water on her face and pulled at a paper towel to dry her hands. "I don't plan to get that close to him."

"Well, you know what they say about the best-made plans. Mr. Hatchet Man wants you in his office. Now."

It's her. Micki's here. Kirk booted up the desktop. The old publisher's password was still registered. He would have to get with personnel about that. Add it to his list. Purge old employees from system access.

When he'd first caught a glimpse of her sitting at her desk, noticed her profile, his insides had twisted with that familiar tug of desire. But when she'd turned, faced him, he'd doubted. Thought his mind was playing games with him. She'd looked…different.

The old computer hummed. The hourglass floated aimlessly on the screen.

Her clothes looked more austere, her hairdo flat and simple, but her scent was the same. He could smell the traces of vanilla shampoo blended with a sweet floral perfume that reminded him of springtime and his grandmother's lilacs. Only the lilacs never filled him with this kind of longing.

The page flickered in front of him. An outdated design practically jumped off the page. A few clicks of the mouse and he knew Harrison had turned off the automatic updates. The man had been working with the best software features available—five years ago.

Apparently the guy didn't believe in basic computer maintenance, either. Growing irritation took over any thoughts of lost liaisons, so much so Kirk almost didn't hear the soft knock at the door. "Come in."

Michelle entered the room and leaned back against the closed door. "Pam said you wanted to see me."

Well, now what? Not only was this the first time he'd ever run into a shipboard companion, this was the first time he'd ever been with someone whose job he would most likely be eliminating. It had been an impulse to send for her. An odd need to reassure himself she was real. Or maybe hope she wasn't. It would certainly make his world easier if this were a different Michelle Bradford. Not his sensual Micki. "I understand you're the local ad manager."

She nodded, but made no effort to move away from the door.

He gestured to the chair in front of his desk. "Pam also mentioned you've been with the company for seven years. Worked your way up from outside sales."

"That's correct." She eased into the seat slowly, stiffly, as though afraid the chair might come to life and bite her. Or maybe she was afraid he would.

"You look good." He'd meant to keep this conversation strictly business. The entire situation needed to remain formal. And although the prim wardrobe, the understated hairdo, and the lack of makeup should have made his intentions easy to carry out, the frightened look in her caramel-colored eyes made him want to ask what happened to his Micki.

Nervous fingers twisted together in her lap. "Thank you. For before, too."

"Before?"

"At my desk, for not letting on we've…met."

Seeing this woman sitting in front of him explained so many things. Sporadic bashfulness the first night of the cruise, parasailing with her bathing suit cover-up, the frightened-doe-caught-in-the-headlights look he would notice just before she'd throw herself into their next adventure with gusto. By the time the cruise had come to an end, those occasional glimpses of the reserved woman now sitting in his office staring at him had disappeared. He should have realized. Somehow, he should have known.

"Yes. Well…" Where was his silver tongue when he needed it? "You're right, of course. Nothing worse than the employee grapevine. I have a lot of work to accomplish in a short amount of time, and it would be better for all around if people weren't gossiping about our personal lives behind our backs."

Fingers stilled, she nodded. "I'm glad you agree a strictly business relationship is for the best."

Is that what he'd just said? An office affair would be nothing but trouble. He couldn't argue with her about that. Then why did he suddenly feel like he'd been sucker punched by the heavyweight champ?

CHAPTER SEVEN

"You're not going to like this." Pam stood at Michelle's desk, her back to the hall.

"The earth's tilted off its axis and is about to collide with Mars." She should be so lucky.

"Steven just stepped off the elevator."

Michelle dropped her pen and grabbed the edge of her desk with both hands. "Is Beth with him?"

Pam shook her head. "But I don't think he's here to place an ad. Thought you'd want a heads-up."

For a split second Michelle contemplated running to the bathroom again. It seemed to be the only place she could avoid the men in her life. If she took off now, she'd be safe in the stall long before Steven worked his way over to her desk.

As much as she hated the idea, she couldn't avoid Steven, or Beth, forever. She might as well get this over with. But she didn't have to face him alone. She handed Pam a file from the pile on her desk. Anything to make her look busy. "Don't go."

"I'll stick like glue." Pam opened the folder, leaned over the desk, and pointed at the middle of the page.

Her finger was still on the same spot when Steven came up beside her. "Hello, Pam, Michelle."

"Steven." Pam nodded, but didn't move.

Shifting his weight, Steven seemed to be having as hard a time facing Michelle as she had looking at him. "I tried calling you at the house."

"We've been busy." *Back Stabber.*

"Glad you took the trip. You look lovely. Tanned. It brings out the color in your cheeks." One corner of his mouth tipped up in an awkward smile.

An urge to wipe the quirky grin off his face rushed through her so quickly she almost didn't recognize it in time to stop herself from smacking him, hard. But she wouldn't give him, or anyone else watching, the satisfaction of falling apart. She could do this. Be the better person. Even if it killed her.

"Congratulations." She smiled, hoping her face didn't crack with the effort. "I hope you and Beth are very happy together, but I'm really busy now." She waved her arm over her desk. "Lots to catch up with. Maybe the three of us can get together another time?" *Like when hell freezes over.*

His gaze wandered across her desk, most likely evaluating the truth of her statement, then settled on Pam. "Could you give us just a minute, please?"

Afraid Pam might tell him exactly where he could go, not that he didn't deserve it, Michelle answered instead. "This really is a bad time. We have a new boss, and everyone is a bit unnerved."

"I only need a few—"

"Hhm hhm." As though the mere mention of his name had conjured him up, Lloyd McEntire appeared behind Pam with a thick stack of papers in one hand. His attention focused on Steven.

For reasons she couldn't begin to explain, the air suddenly seemed heavy with testosterone. From the way Pam straightened, her gaze swinging from man to man, she'd noticed it, too.

The two bucks stared each other down, silently daring the other to challenge their claim. Except neither of them had a claim to anything, especially not her. So what the heck was this posturing all about?

"Mr. McEntire, this is Steven Williams, my fi...a friend." She'd almost said it. After five years, the word *fiancé* rolled too easily off her tongue. "He stopped in to say hi and was just leaving."

The swift dismissal dragged Steven's attention away from her boss and back to her. His glare piercing, possessive, and then she saw it. The moment recognition dawned. His hard stare softened, his stance relaxed. He'd remembered she wasn't his to protect. Apparently old habits were hard to break for everyone.

Her boss extended his hand first. "Nice to meet you."

With a resigned sigh, Steven shook hands. "Same here, but I do need to get back to the bank."

"A teller?" McEntire asked.

Pam choked back a laugh.

"Vice President."

The posturing was back.

"I thought Angie was coming over for dinner?" Corrie dropped into a nearby kitchen chair.

"Another night. She promised her mom she'd help her pick out a new bedroom set."

"Is that what has you all bent out of shape?"

"I'm not bent out of shape. I did groceries."

"Right. And you're slamming the cans around loud enough to be heard on the next block because…?"

"I am not…" Michelle brought the can of chili down with a loud bang and stopped to take a deep breath. "It's been a long day."

"At least you didn't have a chemistry test."

At the moment, being seventeen and worrying over a chemistry test sounded like heaven. "I thought you liked chemistry?"

Corrie looked at her sister as though she'd sprouted a third eye before blowing out an exasperated breath. "No one likes chemistry. That's so lame."

"Since when is science lame?" Michelle folded the paper bag and placed it in the recycling bin. "That kind of thinking isn't going to get you into med school."

Corrie reached for a bag of chips on the counter and tore it open. "I don't want to go to med school."

"What do you mean you don't want to go to med school?" Michelle turned to look at her sister. "And don't eat those, you'll spoil dinner."

"Chill. I'm almost eighteen. Only little kids spoil their dinner."

"Age has nothing to do with it." She snatched the bag away. "You've wanted to be a doctor since Gramma Betty gave you the Operation game on your sixth birthday. What happened to change your mind?"

"I've grown up. Put away kid's stuff."

Since when was practicing medicine *kid's stuff*? Okay, no reason to panic. The key was to not appear upset. Don't give Corrie reason to be contrary. Try and smile. Michelle had faked pleasant and content all day. What was another hour or two? She turned the burner on under the frying pan. "So, what would you like to be?"

"A spy."

Michelle stared at the pound of ground beef in the skillet. Had she heard wrong? "Spy?"

Corrie reached for the bag of chips again. "Yeah."

Of all the battles of the day, the bag of chips were lagging way behind in priority. What the heck should she say to her sister's interest in becoming a spy? *Keep it positive*. Always positive. "Well, that sounds…interesting."

"It's way cool. Think of all the fascinating people I'd meet. Places I'd go. And all for the good of the country."

"Right. So, do you have to go to college to be a spy?"

"Like the CIA will take any dummy off the street." Corrie bit into a crispy chip.

"CIA? I thought you said you wanted to be a spy?"

"Duh. What do you think the CIA is?"

This was not working. In fact, nothing was the way it should be. Maybe if she pretended all was well with the world, all her troubles would simply go away. Or maybe she should buy just one teeny little bottle of Baileys. "How many sloppy joes you want?"

"Two. I'm starved." Corrie flashed a toothy grin, then the phone rang and she bolted over the table to answer. "Hello."

Setting the dinner plates aside, Michelle stepped over to look at the caller ID. Steven Williams. Her throat closed and her palms started to sweat. Shaking her head like a petulant two-year-old, she waved her hands frantically at her sister. She did *not* want to talk to him.

"Gee, she's, uh…in the shower. You know, long day and all. Can I give her a message?"

Michelle bit her lower lip. What little appetite she'd had when she'd gotten home had just left the building.

"Right. I'll tell her. Bye."

"What did he want?"

"*She* wants to speak to you. In person."

"Beth?"

Corrie nodded.

The funny thing was, after seeing Beth at the diner, she was almost worried about her, and she missed her best friend terribly. Right about now the only person she could honestly talk to about Kirk—or Lloyd, the liar—and the cruise, and her sister, and being dumped at the altar, was the person she'd been dumped for. "Do you mind eating alone? I think I'll skip dinner and go take that shower."

Corrie shook her head.

A long steaming shower, a hot cup of tea, and a sappy book would help her tonight. But what the heck would she do when tomorrow came around, and the day after that?

CHAPTER EIGHT

"Where's Pam?"

Lloyd McEntire stood close enough for the scent of his cologne to tease every one of Michelle's senses. All week she'd managed to steer clear of the man. Now he'd come within five feet and her every nerve ending tingled with anticipation. *Stupid sensory memories*.

"Dentist appointment. Usually she leaves notes for Mr. Harrison on his desk calendar."

He looked up from the papers in his hand. For a second she thought he'd only now realized whose desk he was in front of. "I need revenue reports by territory going back eighteen months. I've only got six and can't access the info from the office computer. Who else can get me the numbers?"

"Mr. Harrison wasn't very fond of computers. I can access the information for you. Give me a few minutes to print it up, and I'll bring it to your office."

"Mm." He nodded, and turned on his heel.

Changing screens, she pulled up the revenue data, typed in the time frame, hit Print, and stared at the empty hallway. The man hadn't smiled once since he'd arrived. Not that she wanted him to, and certainly not at her, but this wasn't the same person she'd spent ten days with. *No, you idiot. You spent ten days with Kirk, not Lloyd.*

Hidden behind an unending parade of reports, Kirk…Lloyd, rarely came up for air. If he wasn't buried deep in the financials, or hammering away at his keyboard, he paced his office with the phone glued to one ear. No matter the task, his expression barely changed. Occasionally en route to another department, he'd sweep past her desk, and she would notice a shift from dour to merely glum, but the huge grins and hardy laughs she remembered all too clearly were nowhere to be found.

Every time Michelle turned around, she spied Pam running in one direction or another and always carrying stacks of reports. Before Kir...Lloyd had replaced Mr. Harrison, Pam would be out the door at five on the dot. So far, Pam hadn't seen the street anywhere close to five. And according to Madge at the Corner Cafe, Pam had canceled all her dinner dates for the rest of the week.

On the ship, when Ki...Lloyd told her he worked hard and played hard, she had never imagined this. A stone-faced man who appeared to eat, sleep, and breathe business. According to the grapevine, he stayed in his office till almost midnight every night and only once had he ordered dinner. If you considered ham on rye dinner. Apparently he didn't need sustenance to maintain his fit physique. And why was she going there?

The printer spit out the last page. She clipped the report together and took a fortifying breath. Buried in his work, he probably wouldn't even notice when she stepped into the office. She would knock, set the information he wanted on his desk, and leave quietly. On the other hand, if she simply tossed it across the room from the door, she wouldn't have to deal with the assault on her senses when she got near him.

Still convincing herself that entering Kir...Lloyd's office was no different than if Mr. Harrison were still at the helm, she knocked, entered, and found herself standing beside the sexiest man alive. Strands of jet-black hair stood at odd angles. He must be one of those men who raked his fingers through his hair when he thought, but she wouldn't know that from the ship.

Having fun in the sun, she was the only one to run her fingers through his thick hair. Something inside her pulled and pushed, and her hand reached midway between him and her before she snapped it back to her side. This was not the ship.

Lloyd McEntire dropped his pen on the desk and reached for the papers Michelle held. "This computer is virtually worthless. The techs will be done by Monday. Then Pam can take a breather."

A low-wattage version of his broad smile appeared for a mere second, but the sight made her breath catch.

"What?" He smiled again. A short chortle. If she'd blinked, she would have missed it. "You don't think I know I'm working your friend to death?" He shook his head and pushed away from the desk. "I don't usually impose my work hours on the people around me, but I've had no choice. The data I need is almost completely inaccessible on this technological dinosaur. After tomorrow things will be easier. For everyone."

His gaze dropped to her wrist. Focusing on her dangling charm, his normally stone-faced expression softened. "I'm glad you're wearing it."

Her heart did a two-step. For a split second she spotted a twinkle in his eye. A glimmer of the man she thought she knew. Wasn't that a joke? She'd known Kirk. This was Lloyd.

Uncomfortable with the underlying sentimentality, Michelle turned to leave. She needed to get out of here. Away from him. Whatever they'd had, it had been a fantasy. This was reality. She understood that. But there was one thing she didn't understand. *Why had he lied to her?*

Beth sat at the kitchen table dicing potatoes. She'd already cut up enough Idaho spuds to feed half the block but concentrating on the task at hand gave her something to think of besides how she'd betrayed her best friend. "She won't take my calls."

"What did you expect?" Steven yanked at the knot in his tie. "Sorry."

Focusing on the slicing motion of every stroke, she

fought the urge to cry. "She probably hates me."

Steven didn't say a word. What could he say? There was no excuse for what they'd done. Beth knew it, Steven knew it, and Michelle knew it.

A tear slipped down her cheek. "Do you think she'll ever forgive me?"

"Us. You mean us." His fingers rolled around her shoulders, kneading out the tension.

"No. This is *my* fault. I let this happen. I should have stopped agreeing to help long ago. Every time I stepped in for Michelle at some gala or other, or when she would leave a party early to be home for Corrie and ask me to stay and keep you company, my heart would beat double time. I knew I was falling in love with you, and I didn't stop. I didn't want to stop. I convinced myself there was no harm in stealing a little extra time alone with you. If I had been a good friend, the friend Michelle deserved, I would have let go, made up any excuse to say no. If I'd been stronger, you'd be married to her instead of me, and everyone would be happy."

"Not everyone. You would have been miserable hiding your true feelings. Michelle and I might have been able to continue deceiving ourselves for a while, but the day would have come when we would have realized getting married was a mistake. I love Michelle, I always will, but I'm not *in* love with her. It wouldn't have lasted no matter how hard we pretended."

He crouched in front of his wife, set the knife aside, and took both her hands in his. "I'm sorry. I know this is hard. But you and I agreed with a little time to step back and examine her feelings, Michelle will see that she and I were going with what was expected, not what we really wanted—"

"But—"

"No. I won't let you blame yourself. Maybe rushing off to Vegas was a knee-jerk attempt to avoid my father's wrath, but I still think in time Michelle will accept what you and I had already discovered, if she hasn't already."

Blinking back the tears pooling in her eyes, Beth silently cursed the hormonal rush of emotions and smiled at her husband. Her husband. A dream come true. She loved him so much. Only in her dreams she was the happiest bride in the world, and Michelle was still her best friend. No, this was definitely not a dream. Except for being married to Steven, everything was all wrong.

CHAPTER NINE

"Why not?" Corrie's whining tone grated on Michelle's nerves like a screeching catfight at dawn.

"Corrie, now is not a good time. Our efficiency expert just fired Evelyn and Joyce from human resources. No one expected him to start swinging the ax so soon. We're all running a little crazy trying to make sure we're not next. Let's discuss this when I get home."

"Aren't you listening? The game is *tonight.* I have to have the permission slip turned in by the end of the school day, or I have to ride the bus. That's why I skipped lunch to come here and get you to sign it now."

Michelle tried really hard to ignore what had become her sister's standard sigh-and-roll gesture. The heavy breath blew out at the same time the eyes rolled 180 degrees. She hated it. "I just don't know."

"It's a football game. Not an orgy," Corrie blurted out loud enough for half the floor to hear, including Lloyd McEntire who at this very moment was making his way across the bull pen to Michelle's desk.

"Great," Michelle mumbled. "Just great. Here comes the new boss."

"Is there a problem?" he asked.

"No, none at all." She grabbed her sister by the arm and turned her on her heel. "You'd better get back to school."

"Then I can ride to the game with Brittany and Billy instead of on the bus with all the losers?"

Michelle resisted the urge to do exactly the same thing she hated in her sister, sigh and roll. "No. It won't kill you to ride the bus."

"But—"

"Corrie. You'll be late for class. Go."

Corrie pressed her lips into a fine line, and Michelle knew it was only because her boss stood inches away that her sister stomped off without another word of protest. Though the slamming of her boots with every step shouted her displeasure with the outcome of this little visit loud and clear.

Her boss' gaze shifted from Corrie's departing back to Michelle. "Bit of a temper?"

"A bit. I'm sorry about the outburst."

"Hm."

She could sense the question on the tip of his tongue. "Corrie's my sister."

"Hm." He nodded, a short, curt gesture she'd become used to over the past several days. "Now that I have a complete picture of the operation, it's time to implement changes. I've cut some of the nonessential support staff in HR."

Michelle nodded. What more could she do? Joyce's husband was a lawyer. He made good money so Michelle wasn't too worried for her. But poor Evelyn was a single mom with two kids. Michelle had only one almost-grown sister to worry about and the thought of losing her job in this miserable economy scared her to death. If only newspapers weren't closing their doors across the country faster than the time it took to Google dinosaur, her stomach might not feel all twisted up like a carnival pretzel.

Lloyd McEntire handed her a sheet of paper. "I'm scheduling a meeting with department heads for nine tomorrow morning. I'd like you there."

"No problem." She nodded, unable to force a smile. He'd handed her a meeting agenda. Art department, building services, clerical support, editorial. At least her department wasn't on the list. Surely that was a good sign. Wasn't it?

Why was this so hard? Lloyd McEntire, the new Iacocca, had never had trouble trimming the fat on a sinking company before. For now, Micki's job was safe. The ad sales force was the last department he wanted to cut. For her sake, he wanted them to have time to improve the numbers. To toe the line. To give him a good reason not to reduce her department. Local ad revenues had been dropping steadily. National revenues were currently carrying the burden of the small-town paper.

Tossing the papers he held onto his desk, he slid into the large leather chair and rubbed his hands along his face as though he could simply wipe away all the frustration. Pam could have emailed Micki…Michelle the agenda for tomorrow's meeting along with the others. But he'd wanted to see her, hear her voice. Remember what it was like to stand close to her.

God, why was he torturing himself? He needed to stop thinking of her as his Micki and look at her as Michelle, just another employee. And what was the deal with the sister? Maybe their folks were out of town on a trip or something, and Michelle was doing her due diligence as big sister. He'd had to bite his tongue when she'd told her sister no. As long ago as high school had been, he still remembered how it felt to be left out of the cool group, to feel like you walked around with a big *L* on your forehead. He'd actually felt sorry for the kid. Even if she did have an attitude problem the size of Mount Rushmore.

Kids. Nothing but trouble. He wondered how Dave was doing with the new puppy. According to his computer, it wasn't anywhere near lunchtime yet on the West Coast where Dave lived. What the heck. He tapped his phone and pressed speed dial.

"Dave Griffin."

"How's the puppy doing?"

"Kirk? Is that you, man? At what time is it there…" his voice dwindled a moment. "barely noon where you are?"

They guy always was too smart for his own good, but Kirk didn't have to play along. "How's the dog?"

"The dog?" Dave chuckled. "Did you hit your head?"

"No. One of the staff had a little run-in with her kid sister. It got me thinking about how much trouble kids are, which got me thinking about the test child Deb gave you. How is he?"

"He ate my favorite loafers yesterday, and today he peed on Deb's new Coach handbag. But Rover's still alive."

"I can't believe you named your dog Rover. If you and Deb get around to having real kids, you'll probably name them Dick and Jane."

"It so happens I like the names Dick and Jane." Dave hesitated. "Is something up?"

"The place is a mess."

"Yeah."

"It took over a week to update the computer system. The old publisher still ran things the way the previous owner did—badly."

"That's usually why they bring you in."

"I know."

"Fire the first round yet?" The lighthearted tone had returned to Dave's voice.

"This morning. Two nice ladies from human resources."

"Does this mean Ebenezer is growing a heart?"

"It means I thought I'd check up on my friend. Make one last-ditch effort to keep you out of the trap."

"No thanks." Dave's words carried the lilt of withheld laughter. "I like my trap. And the names Dick and Jane."

"I did my best." Movement on the screen saver caught Kirk's eye. "I'd better get back to the grindstone."

"Right. You sure there's nothing else?"

"Isn't this disaster enough?"

Dave chuckled. "Whatever you say. Keep me posted."

"Will do. Tell Deb I send my love."

Kirk watched a pit bull travel across the screen chewing up icons and slipped his phone into his pocket. He thought of himself as the pit bull, separating the weak from the strong. Discarding the excess.

This place carried the staff of a paper with three times its circulation, maybe more. He had work to do. By the time he finished, the *Bluffview Tribune* would run efficiently with a fraction of its current employees and turn a profit for the first time in what looked to be over ten years. If the Harkness group hadn't bought the paper out three years ago, the original owner would have good-heartedly run the paper into the ground in another year or two at most. Changes had to be made. He hit the tab on the keyboard. Art department was next. He wouldn't think about advertising sales. About Michelle's job. Cutting Michelle's job. Not yet.

"You look like hell." Pam dropped a hip on the corner of Michelle's desk.

"Gee, thanks. You look lovely yourself."

"Seriously. Anyone would think you were the assistant being run ragged the last couple weeks. You still not sleeping?"

"Who said I'm not sleeping?"

"The black rings under your eyes." Pam shrugged. "Corrie might have said something also. I ran into her as she was leaving. You really should consider loosening the reins a little. At some point she's got to learn to spread her wings a bit. You hold on too tight and those wings are going to snap."

"You mean more all-night parties at boys' houses?" She didn't need this. Not now. She was already more rattled by their new boss than she wanted to admit even to herself.

"Doesn't count if the parents are home. I know Kathy Webb. The woman has had a stick up her you-know-what since before you were born. Those kids would have been sorely disappointed if they expected any hanky-panky."

"Yeah, well, an ounce of prevention."

"Could kill the cat."

"That's curiosity."

"Whatever. I'm just saying you might want to take it a little easy on your sister. Let her ride with her friends instead of the school bus. Give her a chance to have some fun. Then take some of that advice for yourself."

"Don't ride the school bus?" She actually felt like smiling at her own joke.

Pam rolled her eyes and came close to sighing like a frustrated teen. "Have some fun. Take all that's happened to you as a sign. You should learn to live a little."

A sign. *Free as a bird.* The thought sprang to mind at the same moment her left hand closed tightly over the golden bird hanging from her other wrist. She'd had her fun.

Pam pushed to her feet. "You're not listening, are you?"

Yeah she was listening. Michelle sighed quietly. But that didn't mean she was going to do anything about it.

"Okay. I give up. For now." Pam pushed to her feet. "But there's a lot to be said for a long night out—if you know what I mean."

"Pam," Lloyd McEntire called from his door. "Where the heck have you been hiding?"

"Gotta run. The captain calls." Pam took off across the way at a fast shuffle. That woman could manage to put a feminine sway into an Olympic sprint.

Two minutes later Pam scurried out of Mr. McEntire's office and hurried up to Michelle's desk. "He just discovered Mr. Harrison's policy of noncancellation, cross-referenced it with the local advertisers. He wants to see you in his office yesterday."

"Why me? I have nothing to do with circulation."

"He didn't say, and I didn't ask. But you'd better go before he starts breathing fire and burns down the building."

Michelle took a deep breath and strode up to the large wooden door. After a quick knock, she turned the knob and poked her head inside. "You wanted to see me."

He waved her in. "Starting now there will be complete interdepartmental communication."

"Yes, sir." Michelle nodded and felt her stomach slip to her feet. *Now what?*

"I have walked into some pretty sloppy operations in my time, but this place takes the cake. No newspaper in the country continues to deliver papers to people who have expired subscriptions."

After a few seconds she realized he was waiting for her

to respond. "Uhm, Mr. FitzGibbons, the previous owner, and Mr. Harrison felt it a gesture of goodwill to continue delivery until the subscriber renewed."

"What planet did these men live on? Why renew if you can get the paper for free? Never mind the problems this creates with the circulation audit."

"Yes, well—"

"And your department. A new contract from a delinquent customer isn't worth the paper it's written on. Belinda's Bakery has been advertising in the Wednesday circular for..." He flipped through some pages on his desk.

"About fifteen years. Since before I came to work at the *Tribune*."

"They haven't paid for over eighteen months!"

"I'm aware of a few problems. Her husband broke his leg two years ago. It healed wrong. He needed a few surgeries. They don't carry insurance—"

"Did all these clients break a leg?" He waved a stack of pages in front of her. "Over five percent of the advertisers are at least one year in arrears."

She tried not to sigh, but the frustrated breath slipped out. "I know, sir."

"And stop calling me *sir*." He whirled around and threw the papers on the desk, leaning over his chair he stabbed at the keyboard. "By nine o'clock tomorrow I want a detailed accounting of every client under contract—"

Pam opened the door and flew into the room. "I'm sorry to interrupt, but this is important." She turned to Michelle. "It's Corrie. County Hospital just called. There's been a car accident."

A fist closed around Michelle's heart. *Not again.* "How...how bad?"

"I don't know. All they told me was the car flipped, and the ambulance just brought in all five passengers."

"How?" she mumbled, looking around for her purse. Her keys. "I have to go." A strong hand wrapped around her arm, and she realized where she was. "I have to get my purse." *The car flipped.* She looked at Pam. "But Corrie was in a bus."

"No, honey."

"Not again." Fear surged, tears pooled rapidly behind her eyes. She blinked madly, scanning the room. "I need my keys."

Pam shook her head. "You shouldn't drive. Tony downstairs is sending the van around."

"No." Lloyd McEntire tightened his hold on her arm. "I'll take you."

CHAPTER TEN

Images of Corrie broken and bleeding flashed over and over in Michelle's mind like the opening menu on a DVD. Her fingers twisted and pulled on a lone tissue. She wouldn't think the worst. She wouldn't. "You didn't have to do this. Tony would have brought me."

"I wanted to." Lloyd McEntire reached across the car and folded his hand over hers. "She'll be all right."

He was being so gentle, considerate, so much like Kirk. He stole a glance in her direction, and she had to force herself to remember—this was not the Kirk she knew. This was Lloyd the liar. The man happy to sleep with her, but unwilling to tell her his real name.

She looked away. "I keep praying."

Pam had told him how to find the hospital, as they'd raced out of the building. To Michelle's amazement, he'd remembered every turn without having to ask her, and now he pulled into a parking spot beside the emergency room doors. Before she could fumble with the handle, he'd circled the car and opened the door for her. "Come on."

Inside, the smell of antiseptic, lemon, and fear smacked her in the face. She hadn't noticed when he'd taken hold of her hand, not until he'd gently nudged her toward the counter.

"We're looking for one of the kids brought in from the car accident."

The lady behind the desk nodded without looking up. Her fingers clacking away at the keyboard. "Just a minute."

"Michelle." The high school principal, Phil Warren, stepped up to them. "I'm so sorry."

She felt her legs wobble beneath her. Did he know

something she didn't? Panic raced through her. "She was supposed to be on the bus." She didn't know why she'd said that; it was all she could think to say besides, *please, dear God*. Her little sister wasn't supposed to be in a carful of teenagers, but in a big safe bus.

From the way the older man looked at her, his brows meeting in a perfect V at the bridge of his nose, she knew something besides five kids in the ER wasn't right. "What?"

"You didn't sign the consent form?" he asked.

Michelle shook her head. A strong arm slipped around her waist. She didn't know whether to lean into Lloyd McEntire's strength or scream at the top of her lungs. This was all one horrible nightmare.

The principal glanced over her shoulder at the unfamiliar man, hesitated a moment, then shifted his attention back to her. "She turned in a consent form to ride with the Webb boy. Someone signed your name."

Before she could respond, Kathy Webb came flying into the ER with a handful of panicked parents beside her. "How are they? Is it serious? They wouldn't tell us over the phone."

The woman was so frantic Michelle could see the beat of her pulse in her neck and the tremble in her hands.

"Calm down, Kathy," the older man said in a soft yet reassuring tone.

Lloyd tapped a hand on the counter. "We need to know the status on the kids who were brought in here. I'm checking on Corrie Bradford."

The woman clacked away, looked up at him, and then a huge smile spread across her face. "Miss Bradford is in exam room B, through the double doors." Still grinning like a schoolgirl, she pointed to her left. "Only immediate family."

"Thank you." He draped an arm around Michelle, and the woman's smile fell like a hundred-pound stone. "Come on."

Without letting go, he maneuvered Michelle through the doors, past the counter, and down a hall to the next-to-last cubicle. The light blue curtains were pulled partly closed, and she found herself reaching for him, for her Kirk, grabbing his hand and squeezing hard. She didn't care who he was or what his name was, she was scared. She needed to move the curtain, but she couldn't bring herself to lift her arms.

"It's okay," he whispered. "You have to be strong." With his free hand he slid the curtain aside and faced a very alive, very annoyed-looking young teen staring up at them.

The second her gaze met Michelle's, Corrie burst into tears. "You told me to take the bus. I signed the paper. No one ever looks at those things. I figured you'd never find out. We'd be back before the bus, and you'd never know. I'm so sorry."

Michelle ran a hand along Corrie's hairline. "You're bleeding."

"I hit something." Corrie sniffled. "I think it was Greg's foot or Amy's shoe. I'm not sure."

"And your wrist?" She lifted her chin, pointing at the splint on her sister's arm.

"They have to make sure it's not broken."

"How is everyone else?"

"I don't know. I was in the backseat. By the time the ambulance came, it was pretty crazy. I think everyone is all right." She wiped a few stray tears from her cheek with her good hand. "But I don't know."

"Okay." Michelle prayed her sister was right. "Tell me what happened."

"Nothing. We weren't speeding or anything. Suddenly Billy swerved, bumped into something, maybe the divider, then the car flipped."

"Cars don't swerve or flip for no reason." She took a deep breath and forged ahead. "Was Billy drinking? Were any of you drinking?"

"No!"

"Drugs? Did you take something? I have to know. Tell me the truth."

"We didn't do *anything*. Brittany was hungry, so we stopped for burgers on the way, otherwise we would have been right behind the bus."

Michelle didn't speak; she wanted to believe her little sister. God how she wanted to believe her, but wasn't that the typical mistake, turning a blind eye to drugs and alcohol?

Corrie must have recognized Michelle's doubts; she leaned forward and grabbed her sister's hand. "Honest. I'm not lying. I don't know what happened, but we weren't drinking. We weren't!"

Before Michelle could say a word, she felt Lloyd sidle up beside her. With the slightest of motions, he barely dipped his head in one of those curt nods she'd grown accustomed to seeing at the office. "I'm sure your sister believes you."

How dare he! It was one thing to insist on driving her to the hospital when anyone else from the office could have brought her, but to stick his two cents into her personal life? He might know how to save a business, but she would stake a year's salary Mr. Thrill-of-Living didn't know squat about raising teenagers.

"You probably scared a good ten years off your sister's life," he continued. "She was too shaken up to drive."

Corrie's eyes dropped to her wrist and more tears rolled down her cheek before she found the nerve to face her sister again. "I really am sorry."

Michelle almost broke into tears herself at the sadness in her sister's eyes. Sitting on the edge of the bed, she pulled Corrie into her arms and held on tight. "The important thing is you're all right. Have they x-rayed your hand yet?"

"No."

"Well, I'm going to go and see what I can find out about the other kids and your X-ray."

Corrie leaned back on the bed and nodded.

"We'll be back in a minute."

As soon as she was out of earshot from Corrie's cubicle, Michelle whirled around at her boss. "Who gave you the right to announce what I do or don't believe? This is none of your business!"

Pulling her closer to him, away from the hallway traffic,

he spoke in that low deep tone that under any other circumstances would have turned her to putty in his hands. "You were about to make a serious mistake."

"What the hell are you talking about?"

"She isn't drunk or on drugs."

"And you know this how? Oh, wait." She raised her hand, palm out. Her tone dripped with sarcasm. "I see, now you're an expert on substance abuse, too?"

"It doesn't take an expert to recognize the signs of a kid who's high. Besides the lack of alcohol on her breath, the fact her speech is clear, and her hands are steady—which lots of kids can drink and fake that—her eyes aren't bloodshot, and her pupils aren't dilated. While Visine can hide the red, there wasn't time to use any. Bottom line, you can't fake pupil dilation. She hasn't taken anything."

Michelle stepped away. Could he be right? Her mind thought back. Were Corrie's eyes clear? She hadn't even thought to look at the pupils. She'd been ready to accuse her sister out of fear of making the same mistake so many deluded parents made. "You're sure?"

He nodded.

Blast. "In that case, thank you."

"You're welcome."

"Miss Bradford?" A young nurse in pink stopped beside Michelle.

"Yes?"

"We're ready to take Corinne to X-ray."

"Can I come with her?"

"If you'd like. It won't take long."

"Thank you. Can you tell me how the rest of the kids are?"

"I'm not permitted to give details but—"

A sobbing woman stepped out of a nearby cubicle. Practically held up by the man beside her, the woman was inconsolable.

Michelle didn't recognize the woman but that didn't mean anything. Had Corrie been wrong? Had one of the kids been seriously injured or... "Oh, heavens. Did something happen to one of Corrie's friends?"

"Oh, no," another nurse said, her tone soft and reassuring. "The passengers riding with your sister are all fine. Minor injuries. Nothing to worry about. But the other driver wasn't as lucky."

"Other?"

The young woman shook her head. "Driver was DOA. Nothing we could do for him."

Michelle gasped and Kirk moved closer. She'd done a good job of putting up a strong front, but he'd been watching her closely since she'd gotten word of the accident, and he could see the little pieces of her shield crumbling away. His arm slid around her waist, his fingers holding her steady beside him. It felt so natural, so right. He wanted to protect her from any more bad news. To make all the unpleasantness go away.

Hand still over her mouth, Michelle hadn't spoken. He could almost hear the questions running through her mind, see her struggling with which one to ask first.

She'd railed him pretty good for butting in before, but at the moment he didn't care. "Are there any other victims?"

"No, thank heavens." The nurse clutched a clipboard closer to her breast. "It's a miracle there weren't more serious injuries. If that young man hadn't reacted quickly, well, I can't tell you the horrors I've seen from head-on collisions."

"Young man?" Michelle asked, her voice barely audible.

"Yes. I overheard him tell the police, he noticed the other car driving erratically just before jumping the median. He was able to swerve out of the way in the nick of time. The two cars bumped briefly causing his car to flip." She sighed. "It could have been so much worse."

"Do they know why the man was out of control?" Kirk asked.

The nurse nodded. "Heart attack. He was clutching his

nitroglycerin pills when the EMTs pulled him from the wreckage. Didn't have a chance to take them."

At that moment, an orderly approached pushing Corrie in a wheelchair. Her eyes took in the two of them standing side by side in the middle of the hall, then settled on his hand around her sister's waist. Michelle couldn't have jumped out of his hold any faster if she'd been blasted with a fire hose.

She grabbed her sister's good hand and turned to him. "Thank you for everything. We'll be fine now. I'm sure I won't have a problem getting a ride home."

He recognized a brush-off when he heard one, especially one as lame as this one. But that didn't mean he had to cooperate. "It's no problem. I'll wait down here for you to get back from X-ray."

Apparently he and half the town had the same idea. Forty minutes later the ER waiting room looked like a packed auditorium. Friends and relatives of all sizes and ages gathered in clusters throughout the large room and down the halls.

Corrie's wrist was only sprained. The rest of the kids got away with scrapes and bruises. As each teen was released, a wave of relieved bystanders filed out of the building.

In a brief phone call while Michelle and Corrie were in X-ray, Kirk had updated Pam, convincing her and some other coworkers it wasn't necessary to come to the hospital. He would stay to drive Michelle and her sister home.

Michelle stood at the nurses' counter signing release papers. Just as she signed the last page, a nurse wheeled Corrie through the double doors, into the lobby, and stopped beside him. The way the kid looked at him, anyone would think somehow all of this had been his fault. When Michelle joined them, her expression mirrored that of her younger sister, and for the first time, he wondered what the heck was he doing here?

Why hadn't he gone back to the office and let someone else sit around waiting to drive them home? A blind fool could see he wasn't welcome. So why had he insisted? Why had he pushed so hard to stay, to help? As the frosty woman had said earlier, this was none of his business.

Forcing a gallant smile, he pulled his keys from his pocket and waved an arm toward the exit. "I'll go ahead and bring the car to the door." He didn't wait for a response. At a fast clip, he was almost running by the time he reached his car. The new question seemed to be: why was he in an all-crazed hurry? Did he desperately want to get away from Michelle Bradford or to be back by her side?

Good grief, what was he doing?

CHAPTER ELEVEN

"I'm really sorry. I swear nothing like this will ever happen again." Corrie looked sideways over her shoulder at her sister.

If only Michelle could believe her. First the lying about an all-night party and now forging her signature on a permission slip. She didn't dare think what mischief would be next. "We'll talk about it later."

Corrie rubbed her good hand gently over the injured wrist a few seconds, and then looked up at her sister again. "How much later before you tell me why your new hunky boss was wrapped all over you in there?"

"He was not wrapped all over me. He was merely being supportive. It wasn't easy learning my only sister had been in an accident and brought to the hospital with no idea if you were alive or…" The word stuck momentarily in her throat. "Dead."

Eyes cast downward, at least her sister looked truly contrite. "I'm sorry."

"I hope you remember that the next time you get a harebrained idea to sneak around."

Her boss's rental pulled to the curb in front of them. If anything more needed to be said, it would have to wait. She just had to hang on to her last nerve long enough to make it home. And then, that man would be gone, her sister would be tucked away safely in bed, and she could slowly, calmly, and completely fall apart.

A few minutes later Lloyd McEntire parked in their driveway, skirted around to the passenger side, and offered his hand to help Corrie out of the car. From the sour expression on Corrie's face, Michelle thought for sure he would be on the receiving end of a teenage lecture on how a sprained wrist did not impede her ability to stand and walk.

Instead Corrie offered a half smile and a meek, "Thanks."

"My pleasure. I'm always willing to help a lady in distress. Especially when her older sister has grounding privileges." Kirk winked and stepped aside to let Corrie pass.

Awkwardness bloomed around them. Michelle knew the polite thing to do was to invite the man inside the house. Extend her appreciation for all he'd done. Except, now that the panic and fear had subsided, having him close only reminded her of things she didn't want to think about. Didn't want to feel. Too many times in the last few hours, glimpses of the thoughtful and caring Kirk she'd known on the ship eclipsed Lloyd McEntire, the hard cold businessman. No, she couldn't handle any more of this man. Not today. "We appreciate all you've done, but—"

"You should stay for dinner." Corrie cut her sister off, beaming as though she'd announced she'd found a cure for cancer. "It's the least we can offer in exchange for having spent so many hours waiting for us at the hospital."

Michelle thought she might pass out on the spot. What was her sister doing? The last thing she wanted was to have this man *in* her house. She was already on sensory overload. Her emotions were holding together by a very thin strand threatening to snap at any moment. She'd come within inches of losing the only family she had. Her best friend in the world, who she'd been dying to call since the first moment she'd been left alone in the X-ray department, was off living the perfect life she was supposed to be living. And now her sister had casually invited the one man who could send her totally over the edge, literally and figuratively, to stay and torture her for the duration of an entire meal.

"Someone just shoot me now," she mumbled.

"Huh?" Corrie, standing closest to Michelle, turned to look at her. "What did you say?"

"I don't think that's a good idea now. You need to rest."

"And I really should get back to work."

Relief washed over her. She needn't have worried he'd want to stay. Work-obsessed Lloyd McEntire didn't take breaks, let alone stop for dinner.

"Yes, of course." Michelle nodded. "Thank you again."

"Yeah, thanks for not letting my sister freak. I really appreciate it, Mr.—"

"McEntire," Michelle provided. "Mr. Lloyd McEntire."

Extending his hand to her kid sister, he smiled. "Call me Kirk."

"Thanks for calling."

Beth slammed down the phone and shot across the room so fast Steven thought for sure the house was on fire. "What's wrong?"

"There's been an accident. Five kids were taken to County Hospital." She opened the hall closet and pulled out a jacket.

Steven hesitated a moment; he didn't get the connection. "Where are you going?"

"To the hospital. Michelle must be frantic." She reached for the keys she kept in the bowl by the entry.

Then it hit him. A fist of emotion squeezed his heart. "Corrie?"

Beth nodded and had the front door open with one foot on the porch before Steven could reach her and pull her back inside. "Stop and take a breath."

"I have to go. She's probably all alone." Beth turned away from him.

Steven tightened his hold on his wife. "No. Think about this a minute. Michelle won't take your phone calls. She practically threw me out of her office. Do you really think showing up at the hospital is going to make her feel any better?"

Beth took a long breath and sagged against the open doorway. "No, I suppose not."

Michelle stared dumbfounded at the man in front of her. Did he have no conscience at all?

"Isn't Kirk an odd nickname for Lloyd?" Corrie asked.

"I suppose it would be, but it works for Kirkland."

The teenager's forehead wrinkled like a Shar-Pei puppy's. "Kirkland?"

Kirk flashed the first real smile Michelle had seen since his arrival in Bluffview, the one that made her heart flutter like a butterfly. With an exaggerated wave of his arm, he bowed at the waist. "Lloyd Kirkland McEntire Jr. at your service."

"Bummer."

"Corrie!" Michelle finally managed to process the conversation.

"Well think about it." Corrie momentarily pressed her lips together and shot her sister that you're-so-dumb glare. If she'd had two good arms, she probably would have crossed them and tapped her toes while she gave her not-so-bright older sister a chance to catch on. "First his parents saddle him with the name Lloyd, and then they tack on a Jr. to boot. Total bummer."

A familiar rumble of laughter met Michelle's ears. Not only was Kirk not annoyed by her sister's comment but an amused twinkle shone bright in his eyes.

"Total bummer," he agreed, still flashing a brilliant smile.

Michelle turned to Kirk, her voice so soft it came out in a near whisper. "Is that really your name?"

"Excuse me?" he asked, his grin slipping.

"Kirk. Is that really your name?"

His eyes turned dark, questioning. For a moment she thought she saw a flash of anger before an emotionless curtain descended. "Only to my friends."

She didn't know which way to turn, which rock to crawl under. She'd assumed the worst of him. That he had intentionally made up a phony name on the ship to deceive her. And worse, now he knew that, too. "We'd be pleased if you'd reconsider. I have a stew slow cooking in the Crock-Pot."

"No. Thank you. I really need to get back to work."

"But you have to eat." Corrie leaned against him, lowered her voice, and mumbled something that brought the laughter back to his eyes.

He glanced up at Michelle, then nodded. "Okay, but I can't stay long. There's a lonesome desk calling my name from across town."

What the heck was he doing here?

Stacks of reports still had to be sifted through, analyzed, and interpreted. He had enough numbers left to crunch to fill a major league stadium. With only twenty-four hours in a day, he didn't need to be wasting even one of them sitting in a kitchen with an employee and her teenage sister. Even if the kid did make him want to laugh out loud. *Besides you can't leave me alone with Siszilla. She'll probably freak out again the minute you drive away.* Siszilla. The kid was probably onto something. No doubt some TV exec will have had the same idea for next season's new guaranteed smash-hit reality show.

He glanced across the table to where Michelle was slicing a loaf of warm bread. She might be a bit hard on the kid, but he didn't think that qualified her for the title of Siszilla. Then again, what did he know about families?

"Corrie, set the table. In the dining room."

A potato chip midway to her mouth, the kid froze. "The dining room?"

"Yes, the dining room." Michelle didn't hesitate or glance up. Clearly she expected her instructions to be followed with no further questions.

To her credit, Corrie barely hesitated before pushing her chair back and stepping over to the counter. She pulled three plates from an upper cupboard, then opened a drawer and set a small pile of silverware atop the stack of dishes, turned to grab a handful of paper napkins from another shelf and then paused.

"Let me." He shot up from his seat at the kitchen table. In half a step he was at her side and scooped up the dinnerware with both hands. "Which way?"

"That way." Corrie pointed across the room, her good arm straight out.

"Thank you." Michelle sighed. "I didn't think."

"No problem." He followed the teenager into the other room and set the dishes on the table. "I gather you don't eat in the dining room that often."

"Hardly ever." She grabbed a fork and knife, and set it beside a plate. "Sometimes on Thanksgiving, or Christmas."

He handed her another set of silverware and waited. He didn't have a whole lot of practice in reading teenage girls, but he knew how to read women. Since girls grow into women, something in the quiet way she moved told him she had more she wanted to say.

"Before we'd eat in here all the time. Not just holidays, but dinner every night." She grabbed the napkins and set one on top of the nearest plate. "Mom used to fold the napkins into pretty shapes. She used real cloth though, not paper."

Used to?

Without looking up, Corrie inched over and placed another napkin. "Do you have a big family?"

"Only child."

She laid the last napkin on the third plate and raised her head to meet his gaze. "Still have your mom and dad?"

He nodded. Though some might consider not having spoken to either parent in over a decade the same as not having them, he knew that wasn't what she was asking.

"Corrie." Michelle walked into the room carrying a large steaming pot. "Bring the bread, please."

Corrie nodded and swept passed him.

He leaned into Michelle. "How long has it been just the two of you?"

"I need a trivet, too," Michelle called over her shoulder

before turning to him. "Seven years."

"Here you go." Corrie hurried into the room, a trivet under one arm and the bread in her good hand. "Okay, guys, I'm famished."

All signs of her earlier melancholy at eating in the dining room seemed to have completely vanished. Corrie prattled on, skipping from one topic to the next. From the bits of information he could glean between breaths, chemistry was a sure A, Coach Davis was an incompetent idiot, and apparently some kid named Billy Webb thinks he's all that and a bag of chips, whatever the heck that meant.

At varying intervals Michelle nodded and smiled, offering encouragement and support, and bristled ever-so-slightly at the mention of Billy Webb. She played the mother role well.

Single mother.

Reports and statistics and dollar signs started dancing about in his head. More jobs were going to be cut. HR was only the beginning. No matter how long he stalled, eventually her job would be absorbed. He would have to fire her. And how the heck was he going to deal with that?

CHAPTER TWELVE

"Thank you. For yesterday." Michelle stood just inside the door of Lloyd Kirkland McEntire's office. She felt two inches tall. How could she have been so wrong?

Kirk swiveled away from his computer to face Michelle. "I'm glad it all turned out well. Your sister's a nice kid. Despite the attitude."

"Well." She turned the doorknob behind her back. "That's all I wanted to say." She pulled the door ajar. "Thank you."

"Have dinner with me?"

She pushed the door closed again. "Excuse me?"

"Dinner. Tonight. You and me." He paused a moment and added, "And your sister."

"Oh, that's very kind of you, but you don't—"

"I'd like to." His voice dropped. "Very much."

And heaven help her, so did she. The man whose company she'd shared on the ship had come out to play at dinnertime. He'd made her laugh and smile, and reminded her how special he'd made her feel. Her fingers clutched at the golden charm. His parting gift.

Maybe. Just dinner. Then again. No. Getting close to the real Kirk could only lead to trouble. Soon he would be leaving for Montserrat, or Kokomo, or for all she knew Timbuktu. Instead of just having her memories of their time together in a different world, if she spent more time with him here, then her memories would creep into her everyday world, and she couldn't handle that. "I'm sorry. Corrie has homework. Finals. We have to work on the holiday decorations. And..."

He raised a hand, palm out. "That's okay. I understand. Maybe another time."

Nodding, she opened the door behind her again. "Yes, thank you. Another time."

Before she could change her mind and run to him screaming yes, yes, yes, Michelle scurried back to her desk and buried her head in the latest sales reports. Why did he have to be so blasted nice? Couldn't he have stayed icy Lloyd?

Having read the same page three times, she finally set the file aside and looked for busy work that wouldn't involve coherent thought.

"I never thought I'd see five o'clock quitting time again." Pam dropped her purse on the corner of Michelle's desk. "You working late?"

"Not me." Michelle hadn't even noticed the time. She must have been staring at the jumble of dismal numbers longer than she thought. "I'm right behind you."

"Want to join Rusty and me for dinner?"

"Thanks for the invite, but I have to cook dinner for Corrie, and I promised her we'd start working on the Christmas lights."

"I really do wish you'd ask one of the guys to help you. The thought of you and Corrie on ladders stringing lights gives me the heebie-jeebies."

Michelle had to laugh. Who said *heebie-jeebies* anymore? "We'll be careful. I promise."

"Well. Maybe Rusty and I will drive by after supper, just in case you need some help."

"Help?" Kirk sauntered up beside Pam and dropped a file on Michelle's desk. "What do you need help with?"

"No—" she started.

"Hanging lights on the house," Pam answered, cutting her off. "At least the Back Stabber used to be good for something. If you ask me, some things were just not meant to be women's work, and climbing on ladders to hang lights along a rooftop is one of them."

With a huff and a good-bye nod, Pam walked away leaving Michelle up close and personal with the man she most wanted to avoid.

"Is she right?"

"Yes and no."

He raised both dark brows.

There wasn't anything that she wanted to share about Steven, the Back Stabber. "Yes, we'll be decorating, but no, even I don't try to hang lights in the cold dark of night." She flashed him her best I'm-faking-comfortable smile. "We'll probably start the project tomorrow."

"I see." He hesitated long enough for her to worry what he might be thinking, but all he finally said was, "I'll see you on Monday."

"Monday." She watched him turn to walk back to his office and blew out a relieved breath, resisting the urge to call back *not if I see you first.*

Visions of Michelle up on a ladder prodded his thoughts most of the evening, well into the night, and followed him through his paperwork this morning. Every instinct Kirk had, told him to stay far away from Michelle Bradford and her sister. The pair was instant family personified. The bill of goods. The trap. And yet, when he stopped to grab a bite to eat after working all morning, he found himself ordering spare ribs, shrimp fried rice, moo goo gai pan, sweet and sour chicken, and beef and broccoli. To go.

Now with enough Chinese food to feed the entire block, Kirk rolled down Michelle's street. No one was in sight, but several large boxes were stacked along the shrubs in the front yard. He parked his car in their driveway and, like the ancient Greeks, approached the front door bearing gifts. Or in this case, food. Though the way to a man's heart was through his stomach was usually applied only to men, years of experience had taught him that good food could go a long way with winning over women, too. *Was that what he wanted? To win her over?*

Sanity, or terror, had him ready to turn around when

Corrie stepped out of the house onto the porch.

"Hey." The screen door slammed shut behind her. "You come to help with the lights?"

"If your sister will let me."

Corrie smiled. "I see Siszilla has struck again."

Kirk smothered a laugh. "I didn't say that. But I did bring food."

Corrie poked her nose into one of the brown bags and sniffed. "Hmm. I say the lights can wait." Relieving him of one of the paper bags, she turned and walked back into the house, shouting for her sister.

"Run next door and ask Angie if she has—" Michelle stopped short in the hall.

Wearing a worn-out Moody Blues sweatshirt over a plaid flannel shirt with faded baggy pants and her hair tied back in a red bandanna, the woman looked absolutely edible. He held out the bag. "I brought lunch."

"Chinese," Corrie offered, as if it weren't obvious from the paper bags and tantalizing aroma of fried rice wafting down the hall.

Michelle ran her hands down the side of her sweatpants before taking the bag from him. "You shouldn't have."

The gentle twitch at the corner of a forced smile told him she wasn't just being polite. She meant it. But after almost four hours at his computer and next to nothing to show for his time, he really did need to come by and see his Micki. He missed her. Missed the feel of her in his arms. The sound of her laugh.

Slowing his gait, he shook off any more thoughts that would get him into serious trouble. Brother, he needed to get this assignment over with. And fast.

"The nail should be just under the ridge of shingles." Michelle pointed to the spot where she used to see Steven reaching when he hung the Christmas lights.

"If there was a nail here before, it's not here now." Kirk

turned in place, lowered a few steps on the ladder, and bowed one swinging arm impersonating a gorilla. "Hand me a new nail and the hammer."

Corrie took off for the porch and reappeared carrying a hammer and a broad smile. "Is Michelle going to have to pay you in bananas?"

"All donations accepted." He clipped her chin with one finger before wrapping his hand around the handle of the hammer and returning to his earlier perch at the top of the ladder.

"Well, it's certainly been a lot more fun hanging lights with you than stuffy Steven."

"Stuffy Steven?"

Michelle noticed him fumble briefly with the cord before she shot her sister a don't-go-there look.

Kirk secured the string of lights to the new nail and leaned over to hook it around the next nail before coming down to move the ladder over.

"So," he asked, climbing back up. "Would this stuffy Steven be the same friend I met at the office not long ago?"

Michelle wished her sister was close enough to kick. "Don't slip." She pointed to the ladder, ignoring the question and urging him back to work.

Stopping halfway up, he turned to glance at Michelle. Memories of a ripped hunk making his way up the rock wall filled her with an unexpected heat. *Darn him.* More recent memories from the hospital of a calm, steady hand urging her on, assuring her all would be well, squeezed her heart. *Double darn.*

Still waiting for an answer, he tossed a glance Corrie's way. His eyes asking the same question.

Shrugging an apologetic shoulder, Corrie offered her sister an overly sweet, it's-not-my-fault-he-asked look. "Tall, skinny guy, sort of good-looking in a metrosexual sort of way?"

Kirk hung another stretch of lights before he answered, "Could be." Descending the ladder he directed another question to Corrie. "Works at a bank?"

"Yep. The Back Stabber. Steven Williams the Fourth."

"The Fourth?" He made a good effort to hide a smile before moving the ladder a few more feet. "That might explain that metrosexual thing."

"Might." Corrie tested another string of lights before passing it on to Kirk.

For the next couple of hours Michelle and Corrie tested lights, changed burned out bulbs, and held the strands so Kirk wouldn't get tangled climbing up and down the ladder.

"I gather you don't need to raid my tool box anymore?" Angie strode across the short stretch of lawn between the two houses. "Who's the hunky handyman?"

"That would be my boss. At least for now."

Angie's eyes circled round. "*That's* the guy who holds your job in the palm of his hand?"

Michelle opened another box of replacement bulbs. "One and the same."

Holding her hand to shade her eyes, Angie watched Kirk and Corrie work. "So why is he stringing your lights?"

Why *was* he stringing her lights? "I think he likes heights."

Hand still on her forehead, Angie closed one eye and cast a sideway glance at Michelle before dragging her attention back to Kirk and Corrie. "He seems to be having a good time."

"They both do. When Steven would help, it was like being in the army. *Do this. Do that. Not here. There.*"

Her ex-fiancé's rigid style and Kirk's thrill-of-living attitude couldn't have been further apart. Occasionally Kirk would look her way and offer a reassuring smile, but mostly he'd laughed at Corrie's jokes, smiled at her efforts to hang the lower lights, and grinned like a fool every time she squealed with excitement at another row of lights turning on. For a man who didn't believe in the American dream, he knew how to do family.

With every strand, Michelle had tried to come up with an excuse not to invite him to stay for supper. But flashes of Kirk from the ship clogged her mind. The man on the ladder was the same lighthearted guy who had encouraged her, had made her feel she could accomplish anything. The one who, despite all her insecurities, never once had made her feel silly or out of place. He'd showed her how to laugh, play, and just enjoy life. Even now, standing in her front yard, he'd done it again. She hadn't felt this alive since…well, since her honeymoon cruise for one.

"They look like they're finished," her neighbor coaxed.

Lost in her thoughts, Michelle had almost forgotten Angie was standing next to her.

"All done." Kirk brushed his hands together and smiled at her before casting his glance at Angie.

"Kirk McEntire this is my neighbor Angie Cannon."

"How do you do?" He extended his hand.

"A pleasure." Angie's cheeks flushed as she stretched her hand out to accept his. "And, on that note, I need to run. My date will be picking me up shortly, and I still haven't changed."

"Nice meeting you." Kirk waved a hand at her.

Hurrying back to her house, Angie smiled over her shoulder and waved back.

Kirk turned his wrist to glance at the time. "Another hour before sundown."

This was it. The moment Michelle had been trying to avoid. Her heart took off at a fast gallop, and her palms were actually sweating. It was all so unfair. Why couldn't Steven have made her heart race and her palms sweat? Why did it have to be this man she couldn't bring herself to say good-bye to?

The last syllable had barely formed in her mind when everything stopped. Her heart, her breath, her hopes, her dreams. *Holy Moses.*

They were right. Steven and Beth had been right. She'd never been in love with Steven. With him her heart never raced the way it did when Kirk came into view. Not even in the sweltering heat waves of August had her palms sweat the way they did when Kirk looked at her with steam in his gaze. And heaven help her, not once in the two years she and Steven dated, or the five years they'd been engaged, had she been so desperate to wrap herself around him that she'd seriously considered ignoring all decorum and making love in a public hallway. *Making love.*

"Oh, my stars," she mumbled, raising her hand to her mouth.

"What?" Kirk and Corrie echoed.

Crud. Had she said that out loud?

"What's wrong?" Corrie asked, moving closer to her sister, a look of earnest concern crinkling her brow.

"Uh. Nothing. It just looks…" She glanced around the yard. Even in the daylight she knew it was going to be fabulous. "Magnificent."

Corrie hugged her sister. "I can hardly wait for sunset to turn them all on. This is way sweeter than what we usually do."

"I just did what you told me," Kirk answered while collecting the empty boxes.

"Yeah." Corrie let go of her sister. "When Steven helped, we always had a nice sprinkling of lights, but this is a way cool explosion of color."

"Glad you approve." He spoke to Corrie, but looked at Michelle.

She knew he was, because she could feel the heat of his gaze burning through her. Everything in her shouted getting close to this man again was a huge mistake. With a capital *H, Huge.* The kind of mistake that, this time, her heart might not survive. She opened her mouth to send him home and heard herself say, "Stay for supper?"

"Dinner was delicious." Kirk picked up his plate and carried it to the sink.

"Glad you liked it."

He lingered at the kitchen counter. "I don't usually get home-cooked meals, and now I've had two in less than a week."

"It's not much compared to all your hard work."

"I had fun. I don't do much for the holidays. This was…nice."

Moping into the room, Corrie tossed her phone onto the table and plopped loudly into the nearest seat. The attitude he'd met that first day in the office was back.

Michelle turned to the sulking teen. "Bad news?"

"No."

"Then what?"

Corrie shrugged, and even Kirk could read the frustration on Michelle's face. Pushing away from the counter, he winked at Michelle, then turned to face Corrie. "Nobody around to hang out with?"

"Everyone's gone rock climbing," she huffed.

"And they didn't invite you?"

"Of course they did." Corrie's spine stiffened, her lips tightened, and the fury in her gaze should have burned a hole through him. "I told Brittany I couldn't go."

"Because of your wrist?" he asked.

"No, it feels much better." Slumped back in the seat, she waved a thumb at her sister. "*She* never lets me go."

Kirk shot Michelle a fast glance, then turned his full attention to Corrie. "Where do your friends climb?"

"At Pete's."

"Pete's?" he repeated.

"Pete's Sports Complex," Michelle added. "They have skating, basketball, batting cages, and rock climbing. The local kids practically live over there."

"So, you're not talking about real rock climbing in the open, but an indoor facility with protective gear, safety lines, all standard precautions?" Kirk addressed Corrie, but the query was directed at Michelle. Since he couldn't come outright and say, "You've done it. You know it's safe," this was the best he could do.

"Yeah." Corrie shrugged. "But Michelle thinks it's too dangerous."

"When was the last time you asked?" Again the question was directed at Corrie but his gaze was locked on Michelle.

Corrie stared at Kirk. Tilting her head, as though it might help her understand better, she mumbled, "Not too long ago." Then shifted her focus to Michelle.

Under her sister's scrutiny, Michelle shifted in place. A vain effort to hide her discomfort. He understood she loved her sister, but the woman needed to cut the kid some slack.

"Can I go with my friends? You know, rock climbing?"

The hopeful look in Corrie's eyes should have been enough to turn the hardest of hearts. Or the most protective of sisters.

"Yeah." Michelle finally nodded. "You can."

The excited teenager practically leaped over the table to hug Michelle. "Thanks, sis."

"You're welcome."

Kirk waited for the expected *Be careful,* but it never came. He bit back a grin. She got it. Mama bear was learning to let go of the cub.

Corrie whirled around and threw her arms around Kirk. "And you, too! I'm not sure exactly how, but I know you had something to do with this."

Taken by surprise with the sudden gush of emotion, Kirk lifted his arms hesitantly and slowly circled them about the teenager. "I, uh…all I did was ask a few pertinent questions."

"Whatever, but thanks." Corrie pulled away. From halfway down the hall she called back, "I'll be home by ten."

As soon as the door latched closed behind her, Michelle turned to Kirk. "Thanks."

"For what?"

Eyes filled with tenderness settled on him. "Everything."

"Sure. No problem." Unsure what more to say, he reached for the last of the dirty dishes.

She stilled his hand with hers. "You've done enough work today. You don't have to do the dishes, too."

"Cooks shouldn't have to clean up."

"This cook does." With a smile, she turned on the water and reached for the dish soap.

Hip braced against the counter, Kirk crossed his arms and wondered what was the whole story behind Michelle/Micki Bradford. "Why does Corrie call Steven

Back Stabber?"

Michelle dropped the dish she'd been rinsing and blinked several times before blowing out a long slow breath. "Steven was my...fiancé."

Swallowing hard, Kirk hid the stab of jealousy that poked at him. "Was?"

Grabbing another dish, Michelle nodded. She ran the plate under the water. Whether she was thinking, hurting, or hiding, he wasn't sure. But he waited.

Hands finally still, her shoulders hunched, she focused on a distant point out the window. "He broke it off three days before the wedding. The cruise was to be our honeymoon."

Three days? *Back Stabber* was too good for him. A slew of four letter words came to mind, all of them too good for him.

Michelle slipped the dish into the machine and reached for another.

Busy work. He understood keeping busy.

"Beth was my best friend. She was supposed to be my maid of honor."

The way she said *supposed to be* pricked him.

"She and Steven were married in Las Vegas."

"Here's your hat, what's your hurry?" he mumbled.

Michelle let the dish drop into the sink and leaning heavily on one elbow, turned to face him. "I never cried. Don't you think a normal person would have cried?"

"Is this a trick question?"

A curt huff that might have been a chuckle slipped past a weak smile. "*Trick* being the key word." She turned her back to the sink. Her arm brushed against his, but neither moved. "I couldn't believe my best friend would do that to me."

"These things happen."

The way her chin tipped up so she could study him made Kirk want to run for cover. She looked all too perceptive.

"Did you lose your best girl to your best friend?"

"Not exactly."

"What exactly?"

"My mother divorced my dad for his best friend."

Straightening to her full height, she cocked her head, continuing to study him. "How old were you?"

"Fifteen." And why did he answer that? He *never* talked of his family with anyone. Not even Dave.

"That couldn't have been easy."

He'd already said more than he'd intended. "Did you suspect something was going on between the back stabber and your best friend?"

Turning back to the window, she shook her head. "Completely blindsided."

Kirk nodded. Wasn't it always that way? "So I was the rebound?"

One corner of her mouth tipped in a lopsided grin. "Something like that."

Leaning in close enough to hear her breathe, he lowered his voice, "Want to do it again?"

Kirk's deep-throated voice sent shivers of anticipation up and down her spine. When Michelle had first heard that sinfully silky voice in the casino, she'd had no idea what he was capable of. Now she knew, and heaven help her, she *so* wanted to do it all again.

Unsure who moved first—and right now, there was very little she *was* sure of, except having his arms wrapped around her felt too good—his lips tasted and caressed. Slowly, with the same tenderness and care a master would use to play a fine-tuned instrument, his fingers soothed, caressed, and swirled gently along the small of her back. The tangle of sensations sent her mind and heart reeling.

Someplace in the back of her mind, flash cards of sanity popped into her head. Kitchen, windows, neighbors. But before her frazzled neurons could process the contrary information, Kirk heaved a heavy breath and easing away, touched his forehead against hers. She really hated it when sanity took over. Maybe he had that angel on his shoulder after all.

There was only so much self control a man could muster and he'd just about reached his limit. His mind knew leaving was best, even if it was the last thing he wanted, but he also knew if he kissed Micki again, he'd want more. So much more. "That was nice, but..."

"I know." Her eyes twinkled and for a second he thought he saw her hands start to reach for him before snapping back to her sides. They both knew standing this close, alone in any room, was treading dangerous waters.

"I have some work to catch up on." He told his legs to retreat but the traitors refused to budge.

"That might be for the best." She didn't look terribly convincing, but she did take a step back.

Finally he managed to retreat a step. "I'll see you Monday morning."

"Yes. Monday." Nodding, she led the way into the foyer.

All he had to do was focus on work for the next twenty-four hours and everything would be well. Except right now he wasn't sure anything would be right again. "So," he came to a stop by the door beside her and did his best to smile. "Monday."

Her hand turned the knob and then she swung around to face him again. "Would you—"

"Yes," he cut her off.

Her cheek dimpled in a knowing smile. "I haven't asked you anything yet."

"Whatever it is, the answer is yes." And for the first time in his life, he didn't care what strings came with the request.

"Join us for brunch tomorrow?"

A broad grin covered his face. "What time?"

"Ten thirty."

With a quick bob of his head, and his smile still in place, Kirk walked out of her house, into his car, and when he arrived at his executive suite, the satisfied grin was still plastered across his face.

After zoning out all morning, playing hooky all afternoon, and then hanging out most of the night, he had a great deal of catching up to do. But even newly upgraded high speed computers at the paper couldn't tempt him to go to the office at this hour. Instead, at his laptop, fingers on the keyboard, he started with email.

Only one offer for him to help an African prince obtain his massive inheritance. The idea that some unsuspecting senior citizen was very possibly going to buy into the scam raised his hackles. At least he was no longer receiving triple-digit offers to enlarge his penis. Clicking on one piece of unsolicited email after another, he stopped at the email from the COO of the conglomerate that now owned the *Bluffview Tribune*.

*Per your original outline...numbers analysis...time frame...cut staff...*and then he saw the words that twisted his gut. *National ad department will absorb the duties of all local personnel.*

Michelle Bradford's reprieve had run out. Monday morning the woman who had turned him inside out was about to get a pink slip.

CHAPTER THIRTEEN

Corrie Bradford skid to a halt in the kitchen doorway. "Wow. You look great."

"Thanks." Playing this light and easy, Michelle poured the batter into the waffle maker.

Her head in the fridge, Corrie grabbed a carton of juice and backed into the room, taking a glass from the cabinet. "When did you go shopping for new clothes?"

"Bought a few things for the trip. Thought I might as well put them to use." Wearing a dark pair of ankle-length capris and a black knit top, Michelle felt like Micki.

"Well I think it's about time you stopped dressing like a dowdy librarian." She took a sip of juice. "I like what you did with your hair, too."

Michelle resisted the urge to pat and primp, but she felt wonderful. Tossing and turning most of the night, she'd dreamed of parasailing, kayaking, and rock wall climbing, then awoke to thoughts of PTA meetings, bake sale committees, and school board campaigns. She didn't like the stodgy person she'd become. Last night, the prim good-example gave way briefly to another side of her and this morning the world did not come to an end. Corrie had not run screaming from the house or taken off with a motorcycle gang. Everything was very normal. Except for the first time in a very long time, Michelle felt alive in her own home.

"Please set the table for three. I invited Kirk to join us."

"I like your boss."

Michelle forked four waffles onto a large dish, then slid the plate into the oven to keep warm. "It was very nice of him to help us out yesterday."

"I think he likes you." Corrie set the table. "And I think you like him."

"Don't go getting any funny ideas. The man is only here temporarily. Once he gets the paper in order, he'll be gone on another project in some other part of the country." Michelle tried really hard not to let her own words burst her happy new view of life. She would deal with that reality later.

"I'm just saying—"

"No. Listen to me. He's a very nice man, but we're not his kind of world. As long as we both remember that, everyone will be very happy." Lord knows she certainly hoped so. A good-sized chunk of her heart wondered if anything would ever seem right again after Kirk McEntire left her world.

Kirk hadn't slept a wink. For years he'd been cutting jobs and turning companies around without ever taking time to consider whose lives he was turning upside down. He couldn't. The key to success in his business was keeping a personal distance from the human factor and focusing on the math. Simple economics. Worked every time. Until now.

Michelle wasn't a number, or a statistic, or data on a flow chart. She was flesh and blood real, and had successfully burrowed under his skin and made herself at home.

"Crap." He banged on the steering wheel and turned into their driveway. He hadn't considered the house very much yesterday. It could use a fresh coat of paint. Some of the hedges were overgrown, but for the most part the house appeared well cared for.

Turning off the engine, he surveyed the home again. Was it paid for? Did she have a mortgage? Did Corrie have a college fund? Was there any place in this little town where Micki could find another job? He pulled the key from the ignition and climbed out of the car.

Whether he liked it or not, he had to tell her what was coming down. He couldn't wait for her to find out at work. "Blast."

As he reached the front porch, his pace slowed. What was he going to say?

Forcing one foot in front of the other, he climbed the porch steps and rang the bell. Through the frosted glass he could make out a perky form bounding toward the door. Corrie. He felt the hint of a smile tug at the corner of his mouth. If you asked him why, he wouldn't be able to give specifics, but he liked her. He really liked the kid.

"Just in time." A bright smile took over her face. "I hope you like waffles."

"Waffles?" Judging from the wonderful smells attacking his senses, he was pretty sure Corrie wasn't referring to the boxed, frozen variety.

Leading the way, she waved him into the kitchen, then dropped into a chair and held up a sample of her sister's culinary achievement. "Sunday special."

Michelle scooped more batter into the piece of kitchen electronics. Glancing at him over her shoulder, she lifted her chin toward the table. "Take a seat."

"Thank you." His gaze followed her about the kitchen, rinsing spoons, putting away ingredients. Some in the cabinets, some in the fridge. She reminded him of Laura Petrie from *The Dick Van Dyke Show*. With the grace of a dancer, she made being a housewife look awfully appealing. The way Michelle's slacks hugged her bottom was enough to make a dead man salivate. What in heaven's name had Steven the Back Stabber been thinking?

"Here you go. Corrie, pass Kirk the sausage and the syrup." Michelle took a seat between him and her sister, and served herself a mound of waffles.

"Hungry?"

She flashed him a toothy grin that made her eyes sparkle. "Starved."

If he didn't know better, he would have sworn she was taunting him. But the Michelle Bradford he'd come to know since arriving in Bluffview wouldn't do that. Not with her sister at the same table. *Would she?*

He had to admit this wasn't the Michelle Bradford who came to work every day at the paper. In her cute pants and cropped top, she looked more like the Micki Bradford he'd known on the ship.

"Where do you go after you're done working here?" Corrie shoved a forkful into her mouth. Michelle coughed, swallowing hard.

"I'm hoping Cairo."

Corrie's eyes rounded. "Egypt?"

Taking another bite, he nodded.

"Wow. How cool is that?"

"I don't know if I'll get the assignment yet. But, yeah, how cool is that?" He reached into his pocket and pulled out a card case. "Here's my contact info. Send me an email when you get a chance, and I'll try and share the fun side of my trip."

Her eyes beamed with delight. "Will do. How long will you be gone?"

"Don't know. Maybe six months. Nine on the outside. Depends on what I find when I get there."

"It must be fun traveling all over the world for work."

"I like it." His gaze caught Michelle's and held. How was he going to tell her?

A horn sounded outside.

Corrie shoved his card in her backpack, pushed away from the table, and leaned over to give her sister a kiss on the cheek. "I'll be home by suppertime."

Michelle bobbed her head. Her eyes following her sister all the way down the hall. Not till the door latched closed behind her did Michelle turn back to her food.

"She's a good kid." He suppressed the urge to reach out and fold her free hand in his.

"Usually. Yeah. I worry a little. Most kids have a mother and a father. Some even have a couple of spares. All she has is me."

"Don't sell yourself short. You've done a good job raising her. It couldn't have been easy."

"I'll admit there were times I didn't have a clue what I was doing. But I had Beth, and Steven." She stood, a dish in each hand.

"I'm sorry."

She shook her head at him. "Don't be. I realized something yesterday. When Steven broke it off, he told me that I didn't really want to marry him. That I was in love with idea of being in love. Getting married. Having a family again." She set the plates in the sink and turned to face him. "He was right. I was upset that my *happily ever after* was gone. That my best friend was gone. That my fiancé was gone. But I didn't feel much about losing Steven the man."

He wanted to reach out and pull her into his arms. Kiss that spot at the back of her ear that made her swoon. But that wasn't what she needed. Not now. Instead, he picked up a few more dishes from the table and handed them to her.

"Thanks." She turned on the water and began rinsing the plates. "I hadn't really thought about it before, but I don't think I could have been with you so soon after the breakup if I had really cared about Steven. You know what I mean?"

He nodded. Micki may have been his for a little while, but Michelle was a forever kind of woman. "It must have been especially tough, him marrying your best friend."

"That part still hurts. But if I look at it honestly, I have to take some of the blame. Until I stopped to think about it, I hadn't realized just how often I'd put Steven off and had asked Beth to stand in for me."

"Somehow I doubt her marrying him was what you had in mind." He handed her some silverware from the table.

She let out a dry chuckle. "No. But I didn't really give the relationship my all, the way I should have. I think Beth and Steven spent more time together than Steven and I did. I can't tell you how many parties I left early, telling Steven and Beth to stay. The bank galas I couldn't attend. The banquets I'd talk Beth into going to so I could go to a PTA meeting or a teacher conference.

"I didn't want to give Corrie the wrong impression

about love and dating, so I followed the rules as though I were also a teenager. Always home by eleven o'clock at the latest. Didn't drink, except maybe New Year's. The list gets really long."

"You sound awfully understanding."

She shrugged one shoulder. "Yeah, well. I wasn't a few weeks ago."

"And now?"

"It still hurts. But not quite so much."

All the plates and utensils rinsed and loaded in the dishwasher, Kirk fumbled for a way to bring up work. Instead, he trimmed the overgrown hedges, replaced the hinge on a caddy-wampus gate, and adjusted the chain on a leaky toilet. He was all set to replace the fasteners on a broken pantry shelf when Michelle leaned over to pick up a stray screw from the floor, and all conscious thought bled out his ears. He had to get a grip.

Thirty minutes later they were cocooned on the sofa, some ancient film noir played on the TV, and he still hadn't told her about her job.

"Is that your phone?" she murmured.

He nodded at the distant sound of the familiar ring tone. He'd left his cell phone in the kitchen. Not wanting to release his hold on Michelle, he decided whoever it was could call him back during business hours.

"Maybe you should see who it is."

"Mm, maybe," he muttered reluctantly. The cell phone stopped, and then Ravel's "Boléro" sounded again.

"Persistent whoever it is." Michelle patted him and nudged him away.

Stomping down the hall, he snatched up the phone and made his way back to the living room. "Hello."

"Kirk?" The timid voice sounded young and nervous.

"Corrie?"

"Shh. Don't let Michelle know it's me."

He turned about in the doorway. "What's the matter?"

"Nothing really, I mean, well—"

"Spit it out. What's wrong?"

"I'm in jail."

"I don't get it. Why did she call you?" Michelle scrambled, reaching for her shoes.

Kirk didn't have an answer, at least not one she'd like. "She doesn't think you'll understand?"

She waved a shoe at him before stepping into it. "And you will?"

"I'm not her mother."

"Neither am I."

"But you are her parental figure."

"I still don't get why she called you. She barely knows you." Michelle slid into her coat and slung her purse over her shoulder.

"I'll drive." Kirk was only a few steps behind her.

She whirled around. "I can drive."

Putting his palms up in a self-defense gesture, he took a step back. There was a time to stand your ground and time to back off. And judging from the look on Michelle's face, he'd be safer backing off. "Fine. You can drive."

He circled around to the passenger side, while Michelle slid into her seat and started the engine. "What else did she say?"

"Very little." Kirk snapped the seat belt in place. "Some kid named Billy—"

"Webb?"

"She didn't say. Only that he brought a bottle and was too plastered to drive. They were just figuring who was going to take Billy home when the cops turned up and hauled them all off to the station."

"Oh, how I hate this." Michelle's grip strangled the steering wheel. "Why were they drinking in the middle of a Sunday afternoon, in the middle of an empty field, in the middle of winter?"

"A party is a party. Especially when you're young. Surely you must remember what it was like, that frustrating age between childhood and adulthood? You don't really need mama's apron strings, but the law says you do."

"I didn't go drinking in fields when I was in high school. Mom always said if you need drugs or alcohol to have a good time, you're in the wrong place with the wrong people. I believed her."

By the time they parked in front of the police station, Michelle had worked herself into a good old-fashioned snit. She was in full overprotective Siszilla mode.

"I'm here for Corrine Bradford." Michelle stood at the front counter.

"Bradford," the officer repeated. "Here we are. Drag racing and underage drinking."

Michelle's face, already etched with worry, went suddenly pale.

His hand on hers, Kirk gave an encouraging squeeze.

"The owner of the land isn't pressing charges for trespassing. And Miss Bradford doesn't appear to have been one of the teens drinking."

Michelle brought a hand to her stomach and nodded.

"If you'll take a seat over there, someone will bring Miss Bradford right out." The officer waved toward a row of wooden benches across the room.

With his hand at the small of her back, Kirk walked beside a still pale Michelle. "Are you feeling okay?"

"I've been better." She took a seat.

Corrie hadn't mentioned the drag racing on the phone. Of course, the conversation was pretty short. But this would explain why the kid didn't want her sister to know.

Staring blankly at the double doors near the front desk, Michelle mumbled,

"Corrie's all I have."

"This is just part of growing up in a small town." At least he hoped so. Having grown up in suburban San Francisco, there hadn't been an abundance of empty fields to tempt restless teens.

"I don't know." Her hand fell to her stomach again.

Before he could offer to find her a glass of water or something to settle her nerves, a bruiser of a cop stepped up in front of them with a downcast Corrie at his side.

"I'm so sorry, sis."

"As well you should be, young lady." Michelle stood up. "I thought we were past this. You promised me…"

In a split second, Michelle's eyes flew open wide. Shock and surprise covered her face. Sticking her arm out to push Corrie away, Michelle barfed all over the floor and the burly officer's shiny shoes.

"I didn't mean to upset her so badly. But I have to admit, getting sick to her stomach sure took the pressure off me." Corrie dipped a tea bag in a mug of hot water.

"Don't think you're off the hook." Kirk leaned against the counter. "Once she gets over her embarrassment of throwing up on the policeman, she's going to want some answers from you."

Corrie blew out a deep sigh. "I know. But I wasn't *in* the races. Just watching."

"And you weren't drinking, just watching your friends drink?"

She shrugged a shoulder and set the soaked tea bag aside.

"Corrie." He couldn't believe he of all people was about to lecture a teenager about caution. "How would you feel right now if, instead of the police taking you to the station for illegal drag racing, the police had to take you to the morgue to identify the burned body of a friend who lost control of his car at ninety miles an hour?"

"That's morbid." She stirred a teaspoon of sugar into the cup.

"That's life. Crap happens. But we don't have to increase the odds of it happening to us by being reckless."

"I told you, I wasn't in the car."

He shot her his best do-I-look-stupid glare.

Her shoulders slumped. All her bravado gone. "My life is so boring. I just wanted a little fun."

"You have plenty of years ahead of you to have fun. Don't try to hurry it along so hard."

Holding the cup of tea, Corrie looked up at him. "She's going to kill me, isn't she?"

"Tell her how you feel. You might be surprised. I'm betting she'll understand more than you think."

"If you're wrong, I want them to play Chris Rice's *Cartoon Song* at my funeral." Without waiting for his response, she turned on her heel and marched into enemy territory armed only with a cup of tea for a peace offering.

He really did like that kid.

Guilt pressed down on him. For the first time in his career, he hated his job.

Pushing away from the counter, he followed Corrie into the other room. Wet towel on her forehead, Michelle still looked much too pale. Now would most definitely not be the time to tell her about her impending unemployment. He could probably stall for a few days.

Not that losing your job on Wednesday was any better than losing it on Monday. But maybe between now and then he could come up with a miracle.

CHAPTER FOURTEEN

In her next lifetime Michelle was going to come back as a cat. Then she could sleep in on Monday mornings. Or maybe a sloth. Didn't they spend their entire lives loafing in trees? In warm countries?

Opening one eye, then the other, she spied the nearby alarm clock. She should have been up thirty minutes ago. Yesterday must have taken a heavier toll on her than she'd thought, because right now she felt as though she'd been run over by a Mack truck. Or two.

Corrie poked her head in the door. "Brittany is picking me up early. We've got a Spanish club meeting before first period."

Michelle sat up to answer and her stomach did a somersault.

"Hey." Corrie rushed into the room. "You okay?"

Head between her knees, Michelle nodded and mumbled, "Remind me next year not to blow off the flu shot."

"Aw, sis." Corrie felt Michelle's forehead. "You don't feel warm. Maybe it's only something you ate. I'll make you a quick cup of chamomile. That'll make you feel better."

"You'll be late for your meeting."

"It takes two minutes to nuke tea. The Spanish club can wait a lousy two minutes." And she was out the door.

If Michelle didn't feel so crummy, she would laugh. Worried all weekend about Corrie, and now it was Corrie mothering Michelle. Maybe she did need to let go. At least a little.

Rising to her feet, she took in a deep calming breath and

waited. The tide rolling back and forth in her stomach seemed to have settled. If the world was on her side, whatever had her tossing her cookies yesterday, and waking up queasy today, would hurry up and run its course. Her job was already on the line. This would not be a good time to call in sick.

"Here you go." Corrie handed her sister the cup. "You look better already."

"Thanks." Taking the tea, she waved her sister off. "Get going. You don't want to be late."

"Don't push yourself. If you don't feel good, stay home."

"Yes, Mother."

Corrie rolled her eyes and darted out the door.

Starting today Michelle was going to give that butterfly a little more room to spread her wings. It only took one sip of the warm brew to send Michelle racing into the bathroom. What little was left in her stomach made its way back up. "Darn it. This is no time to get sick."

The only thing worse than morning breath was vomit breath. She let go of the toilet and opened the cabinet under the sink in search of mouthwash. Soap, Q-tips, baby oil, tampons, shampoo. Where the heck was the mouthwash? Panty shields, nail polish remover, cotton balls, another box of tampons. How many boxes of tampons did a girl need?

Like a flagpole in a lightning storm, reality smacked her back on her rump. *Holy Moses.*

If there was anything more uncomfortable than sitting alone in a ten-by-ten room, wearing nothing but a flimsy robe, knowing you were soon going to be flat on your back with your feet up in stirrups, Michelle didn't know what it was.

So far the only thing that had worked in her favor today was Mrs. Gillimore canceling her eleven o'clock appointment with Dr. Simms. Not that Michelle didn't believe the home pregnancy test she took in the drugstore bathroom, but somehow nothing was truly official until it had your gynecologist's seal of approval.

"Well this is a surprise." Dr. Janet Simms closed the door behind her.

A short, stout woman, she reminded Michelle of Mrs. Klaus without the red suit.

"I certainly didn't expect to see you back this soon after the honeymoon."

She was also probably the only woman in town who hadn't heard about Michelle's solo honeymoon. Though she *was* going to be the first to find out the honeymoon wasn't all that solo after all.

"You're right. The test is positive. You are definitely pregnant."

For the first time in her life Michelle truly understood the old cliché about not knowing whether to laugh or cry.

"I'll want to schedule you for a sonogram right away."

Part of her *happily ever after* plan had included children.

"That will help us determine your due date more accurately."

Someday.

"I'm sure I don't have to tell you the importance of a good diet."

But not today.

"You can pick up a prescription for some prenatal vitamins from the front desk."

And not without a father.

"So. Shall we take a look?"

Dr. Simms might as well have been talking in Greek. After twenty minutes, Michelle had a plastic bag filled with everything the new mother needs to know, and absolutely no memory of a single word the good doctor had uttered after "You are definitely pregnant."

"Here's your prescription." The clerk handed Michelle a piece of paper. "It's very important you take the vitamins every day, as Dr. Simms explained."

Michelle nodded and smiled. At least she thought she smiled. From the surprised look on the woman's face, she might have sneered.

"Your co-pay will be twenty-five dollars."

Co-pay. Insurance. *Good grief.* If she lost her job, she'd lose her insurance. How much did it cost to have a baby without insurance?

Have a baby. Wow. A baby. Her hand fell to her stomach, and a huge grin took over her face until she thought her cheeks would crack. "I'm having a baby."

The nurse on the other side smiled politely. "Yes, you are."

Suddenly overjoyed, Michelle spun around and repeated to the woman approaching the nurse to pay. "I'm having a ba…"

"Yes." Beth the Back Stabber's wife nodded. "I heard."

For the fourth time this morning Kirk found an excuse to walk casually past Michelle's desk. Twice as many times he'd reached for his cell phone. For all the good it would do. He didn't have her number programmed. And why should he? She was an employee. A passing liaison. *Blast..*

"Pam?"

The busy redhead perked up. "Yes, Mr. McEntire?"

"Where is Michelle?"

"She had an appointment." The woman's face was unreadable.

"Is it her sister?"

Pam shook her head, her expression still blank. "She didn't say. Can I help you with something?"

"No. I just thought it might be Corrie."

Pam shook her head again.

"She's a good kid under all the attitude."

This time Pam smiled. "Michelle's done right by her."

"Mm." With his usual departing nod, he escaped to his office. Everything was getting out of hand. He wasn't supposed to be concerned about the jobs he had to cut. Especially not about any one person in particular. And worrying about their extended family was beyond absurd.

So why was he turned inside out with worry? He didn't do worry. Ever.

Twelve thirty. Ten thirty in California. He stabbed at the familiar numbers.

"Griffin here."

"What's Rover eaten now?"

"Two calls from you on one assignment? We must be living right."

"Funny." Kirk glanced toward his door, as if he could will Michelle to materialize.

"Nothing."

"Excuse me?"

"Your question. What's Rover eaten now? Nothing. We bought him a tug-of-war rope and one of those massive bones that's almost as big as he is. Apparently they taste better than my shoes."

"I'm glad. And Deb. How's she doing?"

Dave paused before slowly responding, "She's fine. Is something up?"

"No. This job is just…different from all the others."

"How is that?"

"I've gotten to know the people."

"The people?" Dave drug the last word out as if he'd actually said Martians not people.

Kirk picked up a pencil. "One in particular. And her sister."

"I see."

"The sister, Corrie, she's at that feel-all-grown-up-but-not-legal-yet stage of life, and it's giving Michelle some hard times."

"Michelle?"

"The employee." Kirk rolled the pencil between his fingers.

"How old's the sister?"

"Seventeen."

"And you like her?" There was sincere confusion in Dave's voice.

"She's a good kid. A bit of attitude at time. But, yeah. I like her."

"I see."

"I got the word Saturday. Michelle's entire department is on the hit list."

Dave let out a sharp whistle. "Ouch."

"I worked the numbers most of last night. It makes sense to keep one person on in the department during the transition. That'll buy us at least a month or two."

"Us?" Dave repeated.

"Her. But that's all I can offer. Honestly, I'm not sure after all is said and done if even I can salvage this place."

"Okay, who are you and what have you done with Kirk McEntire?"

"I'm serious." The pencil snapped.

"So am I. Lloyd Kirkland McEntire does *not* doubt his business skills. And he definitely doesn't do women with children. Or kid sisters. You do swinging singles, easy liaisons. Hell, you've even done law students who strip for tuition."

"She's not like that. She's a nice person."

"I see."

"Stop saying that!"

"Sorry, buddy. But I'm delighted to inform you that *you*, Lloyd Kirkland McEntire Jr., have bought the bill of goods." Dave didn't even try to hide his mirth. "Lock, stock, and little sister."

Michelle's gaze dropped to Beth's stomach. Without a coat, Beth's thin frame made it easy to spot the baby bump. "You're pregnant?"

On the verge of tears, Beth offered a feeble nod.

Good heavens. How long had Beth and Steven been *together?* Michelle's mind scrambled back in time calculating how long had it been since *she* had been with Steven. The wedding would have been a month ago. There were so many details coming together the month before a wedding. Corrie had homecoming the month before that.

Start of school was always time-consuming. Corrie was home a lot in the summer. Good grief, she couldn't remember. No wonder he had turned to someone else. "How far along?"

"I'm due May 25th."

Beth was almost four months pregnant. Michelle had been either blinder than a bat or dumber than a post. Or both. How did she not notice something had changed between the two people closest to her for at least three months before the wedding? Taking a step back, she laid a hand to her queasy stomach. "Congratulations, but I have to go."

"Wait." Beth took hold of Michelle's arm. "I have to know. How far along are *you*?"

Michelle's gaze dropped to Beth's hand. She wasn't prepared to deal with any of this. Not here. Not now. "I'm sorry. I have to go."

She left Beth standing in the doctor's office. Her thoughts teetered from dumbfounded revelation of how blind was she really, to *so much for the 99 percent effective birth control rate*, to the bubbling excitement of having a baby, to *Now what?* Pausing frequently on *a baby*.

In the end, fate, or habit, answered *What now?* She found herself parked at the *Tribune*.

This would be good. Work would keep her busy, distracted. Give her some time to adjust. To think. Or not think.

And to see Kirk. Panic washed over her. What was she going to say to him? Slowing her pace, she reconsidered going to work. Perhaps a full day off would be better? No. She'd faced Kirk every day for over two weeks ignoring the white elephant in the room. She could certainly work a little longer ignoring the pink or blue one. Maybe.

Bought the bill of goods. Yes, Michelle was nice. Yes, he liked her sister. Yes, he cared if they became destitute. But he had *not* fallen into the tender trap.

Tapping on his keyboard, Kirk pulled up his email. Distracted by Michelle's unexpected absence today, he'd ignored his email most of the morning. By now he probably had a backup that would stretch clear to Albuquerque. Seventy-two emails. And not a single foreign solicitor among them. Things were looking up.

Departmental reports could be filed. Office supplies, delete. Carbon copy from janitorial services, delete. Thirty emails later, he'd either deleted, answered, or moved the cluttering correspondence. Email thirty-one he hit pay dirt. *We are pleased to inform you your proposal for our upcoming project has been accepted....*

"Yes!" Kirk punched the air then scanned the remainder of the email for pertinent information. Corporate housing would be provided. A car. Driver. Translator. Everything as expected. In two months he would be on his way to Cairo.

He did it. An international project. Soon, he'd be playing with the big boys.

His glance danced over to his office door. His mind turned to the woman who hadn't shown up for work today. Why did Cairo suddenly seem oh so very far away?

CHAPTER FIFTEEN

So much to think about. In the short ride up the elevator, Michelle's to-do list had grown exponentially. What to tell Lloyd Kirkland McEntire Jr. was at the top.

"I didn't think you were ever going to come in." Pam swooped in behind her, whispering in her ear. "McEntire has been prowling like a caged lion. What did you do?"

Michelle froze in place. He couldn't possibly have figured out the same thing she did this morning. Could he? *Nah.* So what if she threw up on a policeman's shoes yesterday. Before leaving to change uniforms, the officer had reassured them she wasn't the first person, nor would she be the last, to do so.

She moved toward her desk. "I can't imagine what he's so anxious about."

"In that case, I think you should know something." Pam leaned a hip on Michelle's desk while she put away her purse.

"If it's not good news, I don't want to know."

The redhead dressed in neon green today, glanced around the office, then leaned in closer. "No one likes bad news, but it's your job, honey."

Oh hell. "Let me sit. Okay, what?"

"Your area is being absorbed by the national ad department. McEntire got the memo Saturday."

Her stomach rolled, and Michelle prayed Pam's shoes would not be her next victim.

"Only this morning," Pam continued, "Harmon called to tell me that McEntire shot a new set of numbers to the board, and you are the sole survivor."

"Sole survivor?"

"You'll be staying on to oversee the transition. Our hatchet man bought you at least a couple more months of employment."

"He did?" Was that the price of a guilty conscience? "What about Jolee?"

Pam shook her head.

"But she has ten years seniority on me?"

Pam shrugged.

Michelle pinched the bridge of her nose. She should have stayed in bed this morning.

"Crap," Pam muttered beside her.

Do I really want to know? "Now what?"

"Back Stabber is getting off the elevator and headed this way. He looks ready to breathe fire."

"Great." Now would be a really good time for the world to stop so she could get off.

Completely ignoring Pam, Steven stormed up to Michelle. "Are you okay?"

"Peachy."

"Then we need to talk."

"Not now. I'm not feeling well."

"I know. Beth called me."

No surprise there. "I also have a job to do. And my desk is no place to have this conversation."

"Then take a break. This is important."

Pam was right. Michelle had never seen Steven look quite so…determined.

"I told you"—she grabbed a file—"now is not a good time."

Steven folded his arms across his chest and leaned against the desk beside Pam. "Then we'll talk while you work, but I can't just walk away without making sure you're all right. I still care about you. Is *whoever* going to be here for you?"

Now he's worried about her being left alone? "News flash. I'm not your responsibility anymore. Go home to your wife."

Like a skinny person sandwiched between two fat

people on a bus, Pam's head turned left then right, sizing up the people on either side of her.

The elevator dinged in the distance and all three heads turned.

Michelle let out a groan. Just what she needed at this circus—Beth. If the woman broke out in tears again, Michelle was climbing under the desk.

Beth nodded a smile at Pam, and shot daggers at Steven, before turning back to Michelle. "I tried calling, but your phone is off."

Rummaging through her purse, Michelle found the phone. "Darn it."

"I brought you a few things." On a mission, Beth opened the cloth bag hanging from her elbow and began removing items. "I guessed you gave up your lunch hour to go to the doctor, so I brought you something to eat."

Like the children in *Mary Poppins*, Pam, Steven, and Michelle watched Beth pull one thing after another from her bag.

She set a drink down in front of Michelle. "It's a vanilla milkshake. You need calcium."

A plastic sandwich container followed. "Tuna. It's wonderful brain food."

"She already has a brain." Pam looked at Beth as though the woman had announced she had returned from a quick visit to the moon.

"Not her brain." Beth sighed. "The baby's."

Pam's mouth dropped open. Her gaze flew to Michelle's still flat tummy, then darted over to Beth, finally landing on Steven. Who at least had the good sense to inch away at the vile glare.

"I know what you're thinking," Beth told Pam. "I was crushed when I heard the news. Even though Steven and I had only slept together that one time, and by accident—"

"You had sex by *accident*?" This time Pam stared at Beth as though she really *had* come back from the moon. Beside her, Steven merely groaned.

"Long story." Beth waved off the question. "My point is, it hurt to think he'd told me they hadn't slept together for months only to have her turn up pregnant, too." Beth spun around to face Michelle. "And then I realized no matter what I had *thought* you must be feeling, the awful hurt I felt this morning *was* how you must be feeling. So, I decided on the spot that our babies are the most important thing. We've gotten through everything else since kindergarten, and we can get through this."

Beth leaned back with a satisfied smile.

She was nuts. That was the only explanation. Or maybe if Michelle closed her eyes really tightly and opened them, she would find herself in bed waiting for the alarm, and all of this would have been some absurd dream.

When she opened her eyes, the dream people were still here. Staring at her.

Grin in place, Beth leaned forward. "It will almost be like having twins. Except they'll have one father and two mothers."

Steven shoved away from the desk, waving his arms at his wife. "Will you please listen to me. I am not the father."

Pam dropped her jaw to speak just as Kirk stepped up beside Steven, his gaze shifting from person to person.

Michelle folded onto the desk, buried her face in her arms, and mumbled, "Just shoot me now."

What in the hell? Hoping to find Michelle back at her desk, Kirk hadn't expected to find a party. Especially with Mr. Back Stabber. "What's going on here?"

Lifting her head high enough to peek up at him, Michelle mumbled, "They're all crazy. Ignore them." Then dropped her head down again.

"Well," Pam started, "Beth just announced—"

"With all due respect," Steven interrupted, "this is a private matter. And none of your business."

"This *is* his office." The petite brunette, who he now understood to be Beth, waved a thumb at him over her shoulder. "If Michelle needs a sick day, it will affect her job."

Ignoring the ex with an attitude, Kirk nudged his way closer to Michelle. "You're sick?"

"No," she muttered, rising up in her seat. "And I have a lot of work to do, so if everyone would please just go away."

Like a pistol at the start of a race, that was all anyone needed to prattle on at the same time. Startled by the sudden outburst of voices, Kirk scrambled to make sense of the situation.

Hands on her hips, Pam growled, "How could you?" at the same time Beth, kept repeating, "Lower your voices, you'll upset her." And the Back Stabber insisted that he "didn't do it." Whatever *it* was.

From there things went downhill fast. All the words and voices tumbled together. Kirk managed to establish Pam was pissed, Beth was worried, the ex claimed innocence, and Michelle, who needed protein, looked ready to heave.

Fingers to his lips, he blew a sharp whistle. "Time out!"

Already having drawn more attention to the overzealous gathering than was prudent in a place of business, he lowered his voice. "Someone had better tell me exactly what is going on before I call security and have everyone escorted out."

Pam actually had the nerve to shoot *him* a dirty look before draping an arm around Michelle and quietly asking, "Is it true, honey? Did the Back Stabber get you pregnant?"

Kirk almost swallowed his tongue. Everyone else just stared in anticipation.

"No." She reached for a pen. "*Now* will you all go away?"

"No?" Beth asked, clearly confused.

Pam on the other hand looked relieved, but the self-serving back stabber just looked smug.

"Pinkie swear." Michelle lifted her hand, holding out her little finger.

Beth linked her pinkie with Michelle's. "But if not Steven, then who?"

And that was the last piece of the puzzle Kirk needed. "You *are* pregnant."

"Look." Steven went from smug to guard dog in a blink. "This really isn't any of your business. If you would just give us all a few minutes—"

"The hell it's not." He turned from Steven to Michelle. What little color she had in her face had now completely bled away, and her hand flew to her mouth. "Are you going to be sick?"

Eyes wide with fright, she barely gave a nod. Those same eyes darted about in search of the wastebasket. Beth's arm shot out of nowhere and shoved a couple crackers at Michelle. Her already ashen face turned a soupy shade of green.

Catapulted by the need to save her, Kirk scooped her into his arms and hurried down the short hall, backed into the restroom, and deposited Michelle in a stall. While she puked what sounded like all the contents of her stomach, he grabbed some paper towels and soaked them in cool water.

When he heard blessed silence, he sat beside her and the toilet, and gathering her close, wiped her mouth with a dry towel, then ran the cool one across her forehead. "Feeling any better?"

Michelle nodded into his shoulder.

The two sat quietly for several minutes until Michelle began to giggle.

"I think I'm missing the humor in this."

Her chest rumbled with laughter. "Really? We are on the floor, snuggling around a toilet bowl, *in* the ladies' room. And you don't see the humor?"

He laughed with her, holding his fingers up in a pinch. "Okay, perhaps a little. How long have you known?"

"Somewhere between puking my brains out this morning and looking for mouthwash, I made the critical connection with nausea and pregnant. My doctor had a cancellation and squeezed me in. That's where I ran into Beth."

"Which would explain the show outside."

Michelle nodded.

"It seems a lot happened to both of us this morning."

"Oh." She lifted her gaze to his. "Are you pregnant, too?"

He laughed again. "Not that I know of. But I got the Cairo contract."

"Really?" Her face brightened, as she pushed herself up. "That's wonderful."

He pulled her back into the fold of his arms. "I'm expected to finish up here in time to report in two months. Three on the outside."

"I know how badly you wanted this. Corrie will be thrilled. She's looking forward to living vicariously through you."

He raked not-so-steady fingers through her hair. "Something else happened to me."

"You *are* an overachiever. Isn't getting pregnant and moving to Cairo enough for one day?"

"Dave informed me I bought a bill of goods."

Palm on his chest, she shoved away to face him. "Bill of goods?"

Nodding, he answered very slowly, "Lock, stock, and little sister."

He saw the exact moment recognition dawned, then he spotted the flicker of indignation in her eyes. Before she could protest, he silenced her with the gentle touch of his finger to her lips.

How could he make her understand she made everything in him come to life? With her, logic and reason were replaced by desire and longing. Dreams of Kokomo, Montserrat, and Cairo gave way to picket fences, dogs named Rover, and babies.

"I'm not going to Cairo," he whispered against her temple.

Tilting her head to meet his gaze, she reached up and rubbed the back of her fingers along his face. "You have to go. It's what you've worked so hard for."

"I've worked hard for what mattered to me. But life is different now. My dreams—"

"You can't let my having a baby stop—"

He held his finger to her lips again. "My dreams have changed, Micki. Before I found myself in the middle of the three-ring circus out there, I had already realized I don't want to have a place to pick up my mail and check phone messages anymore. I want a home. With you. I love you."

Lips parted to speak, Michelle snapped her mouth closed. Her eyes studied his with a laserlike intensity. He prayed she could see the truth in his eyes. He didn't need the thrill of living, he needed her.

Finally, she pressed a gentle kiss to his lips. "I love you, too. But you have to go."

"Ah, excuse me." Pam's voice filtered through from the doorway.

"Ignore her," Michelle muttered. "Maybe she'll go away."

"We're in the bathroom." He reminded her. "The ladies' bathroom."

"Oh, yeah." She bent her head, resting her forehead against his.

"I'm just checking if Michelle is all….oh." Pam missed a step by the stall door. "I, uh, guess everything is…uh…okay then." Backing away, her pace quickened. "I'll just tell everyone that they can go home now."

"We'd better get back to work." Michelle made no effort to move.

He kissed the tip of her nose. "Someone might need the ladies' room,"

"Yeah. We need to tell Corrie you're going to Cairo."

"Staying." He tightened his hold on her.

"Going." She kissed his chin, nibbling her way to the sensitive spot behind his ear.

"Staying." Fingers eager to explore, danced up her sides.

"Going."

"Uh, excuse me. It's me again." They could hear the laughter in Pam's voice. "We really do need the ladies' room back."

CHAPTER SIXTEEN – EPILOGUE

"**S**eniority isn't the point. If the old regime doesn't like it, they are welcome to tender their resignations, but the changes are to be implemented exactly as we designed." Cell phone to his ear, Kirk walked across the room to his desk and laptop. "Kinks in the new systems are to be expected."

According to the computer clock, it was already after midnight in Cairo. Whoever said "When the cat's away, the mice will play" had never met Jeffrey Pierce. Kirk's new international projects manager had seamlessly stepped into Kirk's shoes in every aspect of the deal. Jeffrey had been the perfect solution to keep Kirk where he wanted to be, home with Michelle.

It had always been his plan to expand from a one-man consultant to a fully staffed firm. Landing the Cairo job made moving his plans up a few years all the easier. And to his good luck, the right man, Jeff, had made the expansion happen almost seamlessly.

The one thing he'd learned over the last year or so was that living life was more than working or playing hard, and he was going to do his best to help his protégé avoid the same mistakes he'd made. "Listen, Jeff. All of this can wait till morning Go home, get some shut-eye."

Dave popped his head in through the patio doors. "Are you planning on joining us in this millennium?"

Slipping his phone in his pocket, Kirk smiled. "All done. Did you burn the burgers without me?"

"*Moi*?" Palm on his heart, his longtime friend feigned insult. "The backyard barbecue king?"

"Oh, that's right." He snapped his fingers and followed

Dave outside. "You have a house now. With a backyard."

Deb sidled up to her husband, wound an arm through his, and kissed his cheek. "Isn't it wonderful being neighbors?"

"Works for me!" Bags of chips in one hand and a bottle of ketchup in the other, Michelle stepped onto the patio. When they had finally agreed that, if he hired on help, Kirk could take the job of a lifetime and still spend most of his time in the States with Michelle and the baby, they spent the next month organizing a small wedding and arguing where to base their home and new company. Kirk had offered to stay in Bluffview for Michelle, but too much had happened.

Taking over the barbecue king duties, a spatula in one hand, he pulled Michelle against him with his free hand. Ignoring the people around them, he curled her into his arms and touched his lips to hers. "I love you."

"I love you back," she whispered.

Cheers and catcalls came from across the patio. From the bassinet in the shade, their four month old daughter, Susan Elaine, named for her grandma, chimed in with sweet noises that brought grins and laughter to the family gathering.

Resting his forehead against his wife's, Kirk smiled. "Now, *this* is what I call living."

"Now cut that out you two. You're crushing the chips." A bowl of ranch dip in one hand and a bag of carrots in the other, Pam shook her head at the two not so newlyweds. "You can make kissy face after we all eat."

"Yes, ma'am." Kirk released his hold on his wife and used his now free arm to wave a mock salute.

The whole family scene was almost enough to make Pam want to pack up her bags and move to California. Almost.

Everything had changed so fast. One minute she was welcoming her new good friend home from a singleton honeymoon cruise and the next she was attending that same friend's winter wedding with a few close friends. To Pam's surprise, both Back Stabber and Beth had been invited to the nuptials and even more surprising, gossip hadn't taken over. Everyone in town seemed to feel all was as it should be. There was no way anyone could fuss. As the old saying went, even a blind man could see the love sparking between Kirk and Michelle.

"Where do you want this?" Pam held out the two bowls for Michelle to see.

Michelle tore open the bag of chips she'd brought from the kitchen and dumped it into a nearby empty bowl. "On the table here will be great."

"Easy enough." She set the bowls down. "I ran into Steven at the bank yesterday before leaving for the airport."

"No surprise there," Michelle teased.

"You hear from Beth lately?" Pam had yet to figure out how the four of them had stayed on friendly terms. She knew Michelle and her former best friend exchanged Christmas *and* birthday cards, and probably would for the next twenty years or so.

Michelle nodded. "An invitation to the baby's first birthday party."

"Are you going?"

"Nope. As long as you and Angie are willing to come visit sunny California from time to time, I have no reason to go back. Don't get me wrong, Beth and I will probably laugh and joke at our twenty-fifth high school reunion, but even though I finally understood—in the knick of time— that Steven and I never should have been engaged in the first place, there's no point in looking back."

Corrie came from the kitchen with more condiments in hand. "Are the burgers done? I'm starved."

"You're always starved." As his young sister-in-law walked by Kirk mussed her hair the way he might a small child. Then he laughed when Corrie shot him her standard grown-ups-are-such-dorks eye roll.

"I have to take advantage of decent food while I can get it," the teen huffed, throwing a leg over the bench seating.

Michelle moved a paper plate and jar of pickles in front of her sister. "You're living at Stanford, not Siberia. It's a twenty-minute drive to come home and raid the refrigerator."

"Details." Corrie waved an arm and grabbed a bun. "I want cheese on mine."

"I for one am glad the kid chose Stanford. I'd have gone to visit you in Saskatchewan, but I wouldn't have liked it."

"Saskatchewan?" Kirk frowned at Pam and then casting a quick glance at his wife, blew her a kiss. "Why would anyone want to move there?"

"The minute Corrie had shown me her list of colleges, and I had spotted Stanford as first choice. We knew keeping Kirk's home base near San Francisco was the right thing to do."

Pam still remembered the day Michelle had broken the news to her that they wouldn't be staying in town. Michelle had easily explained that beige and boring Bluffview wasn't all wrong for them because of Steven and Beth lived there, but that Michelle wanted blue skies, pink houses, ocean breezes, and every once in a while, to feel free as a bird. Pam knew what she meant too.

Once upon a time she'd had high hopes for Prince Charming and happily ever after. Then real life had slapped her in the face. Maybe that had something to do with her penchant for bright colors and her efforts to keep life interesting. Though maybe four husbands had been a little too interesting.

"I am certainly glad you chose the bay area." Dave's wife Debbie handed Michelle and Pam a glass of lemonade. "I can't believe how lucky I am that not only did Kirk fall for the perfect woman..."

As if on cue, Kirk reached out for his wife, and arms stretched, the two held hands and squeezed. An innocent glance somehow seemed so intimate that Pam had to drag her gaze away.

"You," Debbie continued, "moved next door to people willing to sell their house to us."

"Well," Kirk tugged his wife closer to him. "I'm pretty sure they would have sold the place to anyone willing to pay the price, so I can't really take credit for that one."

"Sure you can." Michelle grinned at him and inched away. "How are the burgers doing?"

Kirk scooped up a burger with cheese and flipped it onto a plate for Corrie. "For the starving student."

"Finally." She sprang up from the table and practically leapt for the food.

"You'd think no one ever fed the poor kid." Pam set her drink down and picked up a plate. The whole seen was rather reminiscent of an old movie. One of those where friends and neighbors gathered in the back yard. The wives all wore pressed dresses and pearls and the men grilled in button down shirts and long pants.

"See." Grinning, Corrie bit into her burger. "This is delish."

"You're welcome," Kirk said without skipping a beat. He slid the last burger onto a large platter, turned down the grill, and crossing the patio, he cast a leg over the bench and set the stack of burgers on the table for all to serve themselves.

Pam helped herself to a well done burger and took her seat across from the two hosts.

Fingers intertwined, the two stared at each other, a silent conversation taking place. Pam wasn't sure what they were saying, but somewhere between the silent I love yous, she was pretty sure the conversation was punctuated with a happily ever after and a now and forever.

Her heart gave a little kick. Maybe it wasn't too late to believe again in happily ever after.

Kirk gave his wife a quick peck on the lips and putting a burger on an empty plate, gave it to his wife.

Yeah, Pam thought. Maybe it wasn't too late at all.

Enjoy an excerpt from
Honeymoon for Three

When Pam Stuart, formerly Baker, formerly Amadeo, formerly—and briefly—Harris, nee Watson's fiancé Leo suggested a destination wedding, she knew this could be her one shot at romance on a cruise ship.

"What about this?" Angie Cannon, Pam's maid of honor, held up a frilly knee length nightie with capped sleeves, faux fur edges, and too many layers of fabric.

"Ange. I'm not a rock star. All I need is something that can be taken off more easily than it can be put on. And *that* doesn't fit the bill." What Pam really needed was something that made her look ten years younger, not like an over-aged Barbie doll.

Angie cocked a single brow higher than the other. "If you're in such an all fired hurry to take it off I don't see why you bother wearing anything at all."

"Surely by now you've learned that for a man it's all about the chase, even after the I Do's. There has to be at least a little mystery right up to the last second."

"Right. Mystery." Angie rolled her eyes and held out a simple spaghetti strap sheer negligee with swaths of heavier fabric in all the right places. "And this?"

Pam bobbed her head and smiled. "Now you're getting the idea." She added the garment to the growing stack of cruise clothes. The first time she'd married had been for love. At least the closest thing possible to forever love at the ripe old age of eighteen. Each wedding after that had probably leaned more toward hopeful than love, but she'd given each husband her best effort. This time she'd smartened up and done things the old fashioned way. Instead of expecting fireworks and crashing waves, she went for stability, compatibility, and Leo's hefty bank account went a long way toward lifetime security.

Not that he wasn't a nice guy. He was. Very nice. Friendly, funny, charming, not bad looking and a pretty good kisser too. Plus, it certainly worked in her favor that he was royally ticked off at his recent ex trophy wife and looking for a lifetime companion closer to his own age. Pam might not be that close to his age, but she wasn't young enough to be his daughter either and that had counted for something. Her future husband had learned the hard way that reliving his twenties wasn't all it was cracked up to be. Pam wasn't all that sure her twenties had been worth it the first time around.

"I think this about does it." Pam made an awkward effort to raise her garment laden arm. "I can't believe we sail in less than a week."

"I wish it were tomorrow. I am so ready for a little rest and relaxation." Angie beamed. "And maybe a few of those famous Bailey's Banana Coladas Michelle loves so much."

"Now you're talking." Pam laughed at her friend's silly grin. If not for the absurd twist in Pam's former co-worker's wedding plans, Angie and Pam might never have even met. Now Pam couldn't imagine a better best friend. "And who knows, maybe you'll meet the love of your life on board, like Michelle did."

"Fat chance." Angie shook her head. "It will be nice to see her and Kirk again. It's been a while. I just wish they were bringing the baby."

"I can't blame them for leaving her home. I'm sorry Corrie can't come either; that kid sister of Michelle's is growing up nicely. But I think staying home with the baby and letting Michelle and Kirk have a nice vacation is a smart move." Pam's cell sounded off. A sudden jolt zipped through her at the familiar area code. It had been years since she'd spoken with anyone from her hometown. Not since the day she's gone home to bury her father had she set foot in that sorry place, and even then all the old nags had nothing better to do but carry on over ancient history. No. Whoever had the urge to kick up the past was going to have to find someone new to jaw with. She'd heard enough about her sudden marriage and even faster divorce during her last days in Podunk Georgia, no need to listen to any more of it now.

"Who is it?"

"No idea." She rejected the call, sucked in a deep breath, and tossed off the sour memories. Not that the brief marriage had been distasteful, she'd loved Gil and being Mrs. Pamela Harris. But the price of staying married would have been too high—for Gil. "Let's stop at the Bun Shack. I'm feeling a craving for a smothered in onions swiss cheese burger with all the trimmings."

The phone sounded off again, same number. What the heck could they want?

"Sounds like someone really wants to reach you."

And Pam was just curious enough now to want to know why. "Hello."

"Pammy? Is this still your number?"

No one called her Pammy any more. "This is Pam."

"Oh, good. This is Marjorie Lane. I still have your number from when your daddy was sick."

The old lady had been good to Pam's father in those last months. No matter how much of a gossip the old bird was, Pam couldn't bring herself to be rude. "Nice to hear from you, Mrs. Lane."

"Listen, Pammy, it's none of my business but there's been a lot of talk about town."

Oh brother, now what? After all these years, weren't these people tired of talking?

"Seems some fancy law firm from Chicago's been poking their nose around at the county courthouse. Eloise Hannigan says they were wanting records." She paused for one very long moment and Pam wondered if the line had gone dead. Or maybe the old broad had. "The records they wanted were 'bout you. I didn't let on that I might know how to reach you, but I thought I owed it to your Daddy to give you a heads up. You know, for old time's sake. Just in case. Whatever it is, if there's a lawyer involved, it can't be good."

"Thank you, Mrs. Lane. I appreciate the call, but it's probably just a scam. Some prince from Nairobi wants to leave me all his money."

"Well, just the same—"

"I'm sure it's nothing." Pam reminded herself the old gal had been her father's only friend for years after her mother had passed away. "Thanks again."

"Very well. Now that I know this is still your number, I'll let you know if I hear anything more. Take care, dear."

Before Pam could repeat there was nothing to worry about the call had been cut off and she was left with a chill deep in her bones. The last thing she wanted now—so close to her wedding—was a blast from her past.

For Gil Harris there were a lot of good reasons for getting married. Things he was looking forward to. This morning's den of scowling attorneys was not one of them.

"There appears to be a small discrepancy in the current data."

The last time the lawyers had mentioned anything small, it had taken a stack of papers and hours of conversation to resolve. Not for him and Karen, they had no problem with any of the arrangements. But Karen's father was another story. The man had presented Gil with reams of papers to sign before the wedding less than a month away. Today's prenup was to be the last mountain for him to climb. He counted to ten before asking the obvious question, "What's the discrepancy?"

"Your marital status."

"What about it? I'm single."

"No." The lead attorney in the required dark blue suit with the red power tie shook his head.

"Okay, divorced. Same thing for all intents and purposes."

This time all three lawyers shook their heads at him. The uneasy feeling in the pit of his stomach told him this was no joke.

"It seems," the attorney on the left who bore a striking resemblance to the Pillsbury Dough Boy shoved a paper across the conference table, "all is not as you presented."

Gil glanced at the paper in front of him. A copy of his marriage license to Pam. They'd been married all of a few weeks before things began to unravel. When he glanced up, another paper was shoved in front of him. The divorce papers he'd reluctantly signed. The same ones he'd given Karen's attorneys along with his bank statements, tax returns, and blood type. "What is this all about?"

"There's only one signature on the divorce papers."

"That's because that's my copy. The one filed with the courts should have Pam's signature as well." Gil resisted rolling his eyes. He didn't have time for this. "Gentlemen, just give me the final draft of the prenup so Karen and I can move on to the business of getting married."

"And there lies the problem. No county in Georgia has any record of your divorce. You can't marry Karen." Three heads shook and Gil's stomach did a rather clumsy somersault. "Like it or not, you and Pamela Watson are still legally married."

Who would have thought in this day and age of big brother watching and internet tracking that finding one feisty redheaded ex-wife would have been so blasted hard.

"The report is quite thorough considering the short time frame you gave us." After two days of surfing the net searching for a Pamela Elizabeth Watson, Gil finally had to give up and hire a private detective.

At first he'd casually flipped through the multiple pages the PI had provided, quickly scanning the information. Now he was looking more carefully at the details. Pam hadn't had any better luck at picking a husband the second time around. Nor the time after that. Tiny pins pricked at his heart. He'd hoped all this time that she'd found someone to make her as happy as they'd been those first few weeks before everything changed.

Sucking in a deep breath, he set the pages aside. "You're sure this is the right Pam Watson?"

The lanky man across the desk gave a single dip of his chin. "There's a photograph in the envelope."

Photograph? Gil reached for the manila envelope the report had come in and tilted it upside down. A single picture drifted out. The proof of identity he'd asked for. Immediately his gaze fell on the array of colors staring up at him. Pam had always liked bright hues. He'd have thought with time she'd have outgrown her fashion choices, but according to this photo she seemed to have developed quite a flair for standing out.

A smile tugged at one side of his mouth. He'd never known what to expect when he was with Pam, and something told him that would still hold true today. Carefully fingering the edge of the glossy eight by ten, Gil studied it a bit more. A few years older, as was he, but she still looked awfully good. Her eyes held that same twinkle that would have everyone in the room wondering what she knew that they didn't. And her figure was just as slender yet curvy. According to the report, none of her marriages had produced children.

"Thank you very much." He pushed away from his seat and stood. "I'll take it from here."

The PI extended his hand. "Let us know if you need anything else."

Gil remained on his feet until the detective had closed the office door behind him, then slowly he eased back into his seat. Most of the folks back home had gossiped left and right about what had prompted the hasty marriage and almost immediate divorce. The blame always falling squarely on Pam, and she hadn't deserved any of it. Small towns could be vicious against their own. He couldn't blame Pam for moving far away from nowhere Georgia as soon as she could.

By the time he graduated college he hardly ever wanted to go back to that narrow-minded town either. With a master's degree under his belt and a successful career, making time for visiting Porterville, Georgia was no where on his agenda. It was simply easier for his parents to come to him. And now with a pack of nieces and nephews scattered across the countryside, family gatherings were few and far between. Maybe this year, he and Karen would make the time to go to his sister Tammy's for Thanksgiving. It would be the first time in years the entire family would be together, and something about digging through his past in search of Pam had him missing his family more than he'd ever allowed himself to before.

Now he faced a new dilemma. Should he simply pick up the phone and call Pam? There was no time for snail mail. And even if there were, though a lot of years had passed, he didn't want to send a cold, impersonal letter. Setting the photo down with a sigh, he reached for his cell phone. Not the best way to relay complicated news, but there wasn't time for much more.

The truth was he probably wanted to hear her voice a little too much for his own good. Carefully punching in the number highlighted on the first page of the report, Gil sat back in his chair and waited for the call to go through. At the first ring his stomach clenched and he sucked in a deep breath, forcing himself to relax. The second ring sounded and he blew out the breath. The third ring was cut short with a snippy, "Hello."

He didn't need to be an FBI profiler to recognize the woman answering the phone was not pleased with his interruption. She probably thought he was a sales call. "Pam?"

Silence on the other end hung a tad longer than he would have expected. About to announce himself and hope she didn't hang up on him, a softer, weaker voice, responded. "Ye...es?"

There was no way he should be able to recognize her voice on a single, elongated syllable, but nonetheless the brief throaty sound sent his mind whirling back too many years. "Pam, this is Gil. Gil Harris."

Another long pause had him squirming in his seat, wondering if maybe he should have just let the PIs handle this.

"Hi, Gil."

"You sound good." A dumb thing to say, but it was the truth.

Pam let out a nervous laugh. "You can tell that from two words?"

"Yeah," he relaxed, "I can."

"How are you doing?" Her voice came across less stressed, more like what he remembered. Almost as if she cared.

"I'm good. Getting married in a few weeks." No sense in beating around the bush.

"Oh." Slightly higher pitched again, he could once again hear the strained effort in her voice. "That's…nice."

"Which is why I'm calling—"

"To tell me you're getting married?" This time her tone took on the attitude of a wise cracking New Yorker. Not that she'd ever lived in New York. At least the report hadn't said so.

"Well, yes and no," he answered. And just like that he knew this was not something he could just blurt out on the phone, but that didn't help him with what to say next.

"Listen," the single word dripped with impatience, "it's really nice of you to call and reconnect and all. Really. But I'm running around like a chicken with her head cut off. I've got my maid of honor sifting through what suitcase to borrow, two weeks of clothes to narrow down to under fifty pounds worth of luggage without wrinkling the wedding dress, and a fiancé who doesn't understand why I don't have time to see him tonight. Especially if he expects me to get to the port in Miami in time to sail on the *Atlantis* tomorrow. Maybe we can touch base and catch up when I get back."

"You're getting married *again*?" The second his mouth snapped shut, Gil knew he'd made a mistake. If only he could rewind and substitute some other more appropriate comment, like congratulations or best wishes or just about anything else. He didn't have to have spent the last years with Pam to know his tone and choice of words sounded like a judgmental jerk instead of a startled *legal* husband. "I mean—"

"Don't bother. I really don't have time. Let's just say it's been nice and call it a day. I have to go. And congrats on your impending nuptials. Whoever she is, I'm sure she's a lucky girl."

"No—" the call disconnected. "You don't understand," he mumbled into thin air.

Now what? He stared at his phone. Call back? Oh yeah, that would accomplish a lot. Really tick her off so she hangs up on him—again. If she answered at all? Besides there was a bigger problem now than just his impending nuptials. If he turned this over to the PIs to deal with, they might not reach her before the wedding. Letting her commit bigamy was not an option. At least not now that he knew better. Not to mention he had no idea what kind of man she was marrying and if he'd understand the snafu. So where the heck did that leave him?

Atlantis. Port of Miami. Setting his phone on the desk he reached for the keyboard. A few strokes and he had all the information he needed. The *Atlantis* sailed tomorrow at five pm for a two week cruise. Nice. But he had to find a way to fix this fast. All he needed was a few minutes to explain and have her tell him in what county and state she filed the final papers. At least he hoped it would turn out to be that easy. The alternative wasn't going to be fun.

A little more searching and he concluded there were only three or four flights she could possibly be on and still make the sailing. If he caught the first morning flight out of Chicago that would get him to Miami in time to catch her before she left the airport for the port, get his answers, and be back home before Karen even noticed he was gone. At least he certainly hoped so. Otherwise he was going to have two very unhappy women on his hands.

On the deck ready to wave Miami goodbye, Pam watched the crowds still boarding the ship.

"Is Leo on board yet?" Angie asked, her nose to the air, sucking up the Florida sunshine.

"From the minute they let the new passengers on the boat. You know him, always first in line. He's already settled in the suite."

"I think it's kinda sweet that you're not sharing a cabin until after the wedding in St. Marteen. Sort of romantic."

That was the plan. "Figured this time if I'm going for old fashioned, I'm going to do everything right. Besides, I think it's getting Leo all fired up, and that will be fun."

Angie's phone clinked. "Oh, Michelle and Kirk just checked into their rooms. They're going to grab lunch upstairs. They want to know if we'd like to join them."

Pam would rather watch the crowds and bask a short while longer in the Miami heat. She certainly understood why folks migrated south. She'd love to move into a cabin on a cruise ship and just keep sailing. "You can't be hungry."

"No, not really." Angie leaned more heavily on the railing. "It's still early by my clock."

"The two six-inch Subway sandwiches you scarfed down at the airport probably didn't hurt any."

Biting back a sweet smile, Angie shrugged. "I didn't have time for breakfast before we left the house."

A couple of guys leaned over the railing beside Pam. Not bad looking, the question of course was whether they were here together or *together*. Not that it mattered, she was off the market. But Angie could use a little fun in her life. She was too young to be cloistered at home working late hours almost every day of the week. The few times Pam could drag her out of the house it was only for dinner or a movie. Her friend hardly every joined her at the nightspots for a drink or dancing. Pam really hoped this cruise would loosen her up at bit.

"Looks like we're going to have great weather," the taller fellow with the sandy blonde hair said in her direction.

"Is there such a thing as bad weather in Florida?" Pam tilted her head, studying the two men.

"Depends on whether or not you like rain." The blonde stuck his hand out. "I'm Brian Reynolds, this here is my brother Taylor."

"Nice to meet you." She extended her hand as well. "I'm Pam, and this is my friend Angie."

"You ladies traveling alone?" Taylor asked, as though deciding this talking to strangers wasn't such a bad idea.

"There are a few more friends joining us. This is my wedding cruise."

"Congratulations." For a split second she thought she saw a flicker of disappointment in Blondie's eyes, but that couldn't be, she had a few good years on him. "Great venue for a wedding."

"Angie is my maid of honor. My fiancé's brother is standing up for him. He brought his wife and two kids. My best friend and her husband are joining us from California. Small and intimate." Pam noticed Taylor glancing at Angie. Maybe this cruise thing could work out for Angie after all. "Just the seven of us and the kids."

"They're not really kids. They're in college." Angie added, oblivious to Taylor's interest.

"Sounds like fun just the same." Blondie's smile seemed genuine.

Another place and time and getting to know Blondie better would have been appealing. But not any more. Pam was settling down for real this time. Her cell phone sounded off and she didn't bother to look at the caller ID. "Must be Michelle wanting to convince us to go eat, like there's not going to be food twenty-four seven for the next two weeks. Hello."

"Pam."

One syllable and she knew the voice. After all these years how could one word from one man still make her toes tingle. She stepped away from Angie, turning her back to the now chatting new friends. "Gil, I thought we agreed that there was nothing to say."

"Actually, we didn't. There's something very important for me to say to you. But I'd rather do it in person. Are you still here at the airport?"

Pam glanced around. What did he mean by *here*? "No. I told you. I'm sailing on my wedding cruise." She took two more steps away. "Listen, Gil. I'm flattered you want to visit. But this is simply not a good time. I really have to go."

"Don't hang up! Please."

She almost did exactly that, but something almost desperate in his tone stopped her.

"Pam, I need to know where you filed the divorce papers. What county?"

"Where did *I* file the papers?"

"That's what I said."

"I didn't file anything. I signed the papers my lawyer gave me. His assistant told me that after you signed your lawyer would file. Ask him where he did it."

The acid churning in Gil's stomach for the last couple of hours as it finally dawned on him that he'd missed Pam at the airport was now on fire. Someone somewhere had things back asswards. The way he remembered the situation going down was that he signed a copy, and his attorney was giving it to Pam's attorney for her to sign, and then she and her attorney were to file the papers. He never saw anything with her signature on it. "Pam, are you sure?"

"What do you mean, am I sure? I sat in the lawyer's office. Signed on the dotted line and left."

Slinging his carryon bag over his shoulder, he bypassed the baggage claim area and headed toward the taxi stand area. "This is really important, Pam." He had to take a deep breath himself to stay calm. "Was my signature on those papers?"

"I'm not a senile old lady, Gil. I don't have to think hard. I remember that day like it was yesterday. It's not the same as an ordinary day of going to the grocery store for milk and bread. Things like signing divorce papers have a way of sticking with you. Mr. Henry's legal assistant pulled the pages off the printer, set them in front of me and showed me where to sign. Mine was the only signature."

Gil stopped walking. Pinching the bridge of his nose he couldn't think of any way that would be a good way to say this. "I want you to stay calm, but if what you say is correct, and I have no reason to doubt you, then there's trouble in paradise."

"What kind of trouble?" The hint of anger in her earlier tone slipped away giving in to a nervous crack.

"Pam, we're still married."

MEET CHRIS

Author of dozens of contemporary novels, including the award winning Aloha Series, Chris Keniston lives in suburban Dallas with her husband, two human children, and two canine children. Though she loves her puppies equally, she admits being especially attached to her German Shepherd rescue. After all, even dogs deserve a happily ever after.

More on Chris and her books can be found at
www.chriskeniston.com

Follow Chris on Facebook at ChrisKenistonAuthor
or on Twitter @ckenistonauthor

Questions? Comments?
I would love to hear from you.
You can reach me at chris@chriskeniston.com